ICEBOUND

Legends of the Shifters

Book Two

By J.B. North

Icebound (Legends of the Shifters: Book Two)

Copyright © 2015 by J.B. North

Cover art by Widhi Saputro

ISBN-13: 978-1517433161

ISBN-10: 1517433169

For Aunt Kristy,

the book fanatic who inspired me to read.

Chapter One

I CY RAIN POURED from the foreboding clouds, drenching and darkening the color of my fiery feathers. I squinted through the rain, wavering with the extra weight of water on my already exhausted body. But I couldn't stop. I had to get to King Ciaran's castle. My brother was still in there, wasting away in a rat-infested cell…if he wasn't already dead.

I remembered seeing the bodies down there. The ones that were too still and stinking to be alive. *I won't let him be one of them.*

I just hoped he was hanging on until I could help him escape.

It had been two days since I left the Isle of Ginsey. I hadn't stopped once, even though my wings begged me to give up and land.

I can't give in. Not until I see the turrets of the castle.

My jaw ached from gripping the plant of eternal life as delicately as I could. I was tempted to drop it, to watch the rain batter it as it tumbled to the ground, but I couldn't bring myself to open my beak. Roland died so I could have the plant. To let it slip away would betray his dying wish.

I pushed through the rain, but my muscles threatened to give up on me, stiff with cold and overuse. Darkness tinged the corners of my vision. I shook my head to keep awake.

Then, I caught a glimpse of the walls that surrounded the city of King's Crest. Relief swept over me. I finally made it.

I would have liked to press on to get to Kurt, but my wings refused to hold me for much longer. I sailed downward, forcing my eyes to stay open as I landed heavily on a wooded hillside.

Breathless, I shifted form for the first time in days. After being in the phoenix body for so long, my knees trembled beneath my weight.

I let the plant drop to the ground on the leaves beside me as I sunk against a tree trunk. I was soaked and cold, but my body had already decided to shut down. Before I faded out completely, I reached over and clutched the plant in my hand.

It was as if I were holding a piece of the sun. Heat coursed through my body, flooding me with calm.

Maybe Roland was looking down on me right then, from the "forever" he had talked about. Maybe the brilliant angel that he'd mentioned was standing next to him, keeping me safe.

I let that thought comfort me as I closed my eyes.

Tomorrow. I would try to find Kurt tomorrow.

❖   ❖   ❖

I awoke to pain, but it wasn't just the soreness that cramped every single muscle in my body.

It was a ripping feeling in my chest, as if someone was slowly dragging a serrated knife through my heart. I managed to open my eyes long enough to see that there was no one around me and no blade stuck through my chest. The strange pain I felt came from the inside.

I curled into a tight ball, holding back a tortured cry as best I could. If there were sentries nearby, the last thing I wanted them to know was that I existed and that I was weak. I wouldn't be able to defend myself while enduring a pain this excruciating.

The invisible knife traveled upward, dragging along my collarbone and creeping down my shoulder. I squeezed my eyes closed, waiting for the pain to ebb.

Then, just as quickly as it had come, it was gone, leaving me gasping for air.

I lay motionless for a while, giving myself time to catch my breath. I stared at my trembling hand in the fallen leaves, deeply breathing in the soothing scent of damp earth. It took a few moments to summon the courage to push myself to my knees, but I did eventually, trusting that movement wouldn't trigger the pain again.

I pulled my sleeve to the side and studied the scar that now zig-zagged over my freckles with a grimace. I ran my finger along the ugly, jagged line. The area was so numb I could barely feel the touch. I sat back, horrified. What could possibly have made this scar appear?

Only one thing came to mind.

Frantically, I looked around for the plant. It took seconds to realize that I still had it clutched safely in my hand, but I uncurled my fingers to find them somewhat sticky with clear, greenish goop. The stem of the plant was slightly nicked and bruised where my beak had clamped down on it. With a sinking feeling in my stomach, I understood what had happened. I'd severed it when I landed clumsily the night before.

For a moment, everything—the wind rustling the leaves, the birds singing, even my own breathing—went silent. I just stared at the little plant, studying how the flowers were starting to curl and turn brown at the ends.

A pang shot through my heart, deeper than any physical hurt. This plant should have been for Roland. Its power wasn't supposed to be running through *my* blood. And did this mean I was immortal?

As I took in a few steadying breaths, the scar began to tingle, pins and needles running along the length of it. I expected the pain to kick in again, but instead, my body began to feel lighter. The sensation was much like what I'd felt a few days ago, when I'd been granted strength to beat the iron giant.

The plant was already making me stronger.

I raised a shaking hand to my forehead. *It can't mean I'm immortal.*

After witnessing the angels in the fourth and final test and Roland's last breath, the swing of death's scythe barely intimidated me. And yet, I knew my life could be used for good. Kurt was still trapped, my friends still waited for my return to the conservatory, and I still had a prophecy to fulfill, whatever it may be.

But forever is a long time.

My spinning thoughts came to a halt when I heard a whisper of movement. I listened closely, but it seemed like my pounding heart drowned out the world.

Then, leaves rustled behind me, too forceful to be wind. I spun around.

Three guards stood there, one woman, two men, their crossbows pointed directly at my chest. They moved smoothly, circling me.

I held my hands in the air, feeling the pressure of three sharp arrow tips, though each of them were five feet away. "What do you want?" The only sign of my distress was the high-pitched crack in the last word.

The woman narrowed her eyes. "We need you to come with us."

I refused to be captured by King Ciaran's men. Not again.

I shifted into half-form and tucked the plant away in my pocket, where my mother's necklace still hid.

"Hands up! Don't move!"

Power surged through me as I looked back up, my anger rising. "*No.*"

The air reverberated with tension and the sound of ringing metal as I drew my sword and struck at the nearest guard's weapon. I managed to take him by surprise, sending the bow hurtling a few yards away.

Whatever satisfaction I felt wasn't long-lived. I heard the click of a crossbow as it released an arrow and watched out of the corner of my eye as the whistling spear spun toward me, sinking deep into the flesh of my left arm. I bit back a cry, my sword thudding to the ground. The seething anger that coursed through my blood somehow managed to diminish the pain as I pulled the arrow out of my arm, growling through the agony.

The woman eyed me warily. "This can end now. Don't put up a fight and I guarantee you'll live another day."

I dropped the blood-tipped arrow to the ground. "I'm *not* coming with you."

And then she pulled the trigger.

Without even thinking, I reacted, catching the arrow right before it plunged through my ribs.

The three guards stared at me with wide eyes as I panted, and before anyone could do anything else, I tossed the arrow away and swept down to retrieve my sword. Now the woman had her own blade drawn, a wicked looking thing that resembled a curved machete.

I flew into action, first attacking the man whose arrow had pierced my flesh, releasing all of my energy into a blow across the metal breastplate that protected his chest. To my surprise, my blade cut cleanly through the armor and into his torso. With a strangled cry, the guard crumpled to the ground. Had I used normal human strength, the blow would have delivered a dent and a bruise, not death.

In the back of my mind, a single thought kept running through my head. *I just killed a man. I killed him.*

I didn't have time to think about it. Not yet.

I turned to the other guards and advanced. The woman struck at me first, so I parried the attack to the side before I grabbed her sword arm, stepped in close where her weapon wouldn't reach, and elbowed her in the temple hard enough to render her unconscious, but not dead.

For goodness sake, I hoped that she wasn't dead.

She thumped to the ground behind me as I turned to the last guard, the one that I'd struck at first.

His hands were shaking as he fumbled to reload his crossbow, having already pulled the string taut, but still attempting to get the arrow into position. I jerked the bow out of his hands and rested my blade against his throat. His Adam's apple bobbed against the metal as he swallowed tightly, eyes wild with fear.

"What does your king want with me?" I interrogated.

He took in a shaky breath. "The king's borders mark you as a foreigner. Foreigners must be captured and brought to the king."

I narrowed my eyes. Borders?

"Not this one," I replied, and with the hilt of my sword, I knocked him out cold. He collapsed to the ground.

I stood back and looked around, the reality of the situation finally settling in. I'd just injured two strangers and killed one.

Before this, I hadn't killed anyone. I stared at the dead guard for a while, bile rising up in my throat.

That man had a life, and I took it with one swipe of my sword. What if he had a family that loved him? A wife and children?

I banished the thought. It was too much for my already aching heart.

My arm wound helped to distract me. The throbbing pain was diminishing quickly, a sure sign that the plant's power was doing its job. As I watched, the rip in my flesh slowly knitted back together until the only proof of its former existence was the crimson stain that still soaked my arm and my dress. I sighed with relief when the pain went with it.

I searched each guard's bags for anything of value and found a small amount of food and some coins. I was about to leave them when an idea formed in my head.

The woman couldn't have been that much bigger than me. If I were to dress up like a Ginsian guard, it may smooth over my attempt to get into the castle undetected.

It was the best plan I'd come up with yet.

I made my way back over to the woman and began to strip her armor, scanning the forest for anyone else that might be lurking about. There was no one in sight, human or animal.

Once I shifted back into first form and had all the armor in place, I continued toward the wall of the city. There was no gate nearby, so I trailed along the crumbling stone, snacking on the bread and cheese I'd stolen from the guards. I never found an actual entrance, but there was a section that seemed easier than the rest to scale. I climbed over the mess of eroded rocks and dropped to the other side, squinting through the trees. I could just make out a cluster of buildings.

I ran forward, armor clanking with every stride. The woman's boots were the only thing too big for me, but by curling up my toes, I managed to keep them on. I rounded one of the buildings, and made it to the cobblestone of the city street. To avoid the attention of the commoners, I slowed to a quick walk.

As I passed a man and his child, they cowered away, eyes averted. Most people skirted around me, some even disappearing down alleyways before I got to them. As I neared the castle gate, the number of villagers dwindled, replaced by more soldiers than I've ever seen in one place before. The gate itself wasn't surrounded by beggars like before, but was instead guarded heavily by rows of armored individuals.

I steeled myself as I walked past the lines of guards. I kept feeling like someone would stop me at any moment, but surprisingly, I got through without any questions. I passed through the gap in the gate and focused on the castle ahead. Unlike the last time I'd been here, a large black flag hung on the stone of the castle that read:

WE WILL CONQUER.

I shuddered and skirted around a statue of King Ciaran that was being chiseled out of rock.

As I climbed the steps to the large front doors, I counted seven guards crowded around it, standing silently side by side. I strode forward boldly

The guard in front stepped toward me. "What is it, soldier?"

"The commander sent me to guard the corridor," I replied, hoping that would be enough.

The man scrutinized me, eyes searching my face. Eventually, he shook his head and grumbled, "We'll let you through this once, but you need to go through the east entrance from now on."

He motioned to the other guards, and three of them moved away from the door to let me through.

"Beginners," one of them snickered to the other.

On the other side, two more guards stood beside the door. I nodded to them and continued walking down the hall.

The memory of being led to the dungeons by King Ciaran seemed cemented in my mind, so it wasn't hard to navigate the castle.

I erased all emotion from my face when a couple guards hurried past, their armor clanking. I managed to hear a few words of their conversation.

"—castle has been breached. The king says there is someone very powerful within the walls—"

I turned right, into another corridor, my mind spinning. Could King Ciaran sense my presence? If so, he couldn't be very far away. I'd only entered the castle seconds ago.

I picked up my pace, palms sweating. The dungeon door was the last on the left, but there was definitely something off about it.

Then I realized—no guards. I hesitated outside for a moment, wondering if I should go through with my plan.

No. I didn't come this far just to turn away. I reached forward and grabbed the handle. Unlocked.

I pushed the door open, and let my eyes adjust to the darkness as I shut it behind me and turned the lock into place.

Blood rushed in my ears as I waited in the darkness. I took a step forward, but something rattled along the ground. Something I'd kicked. I squinted my eyes and peered closer.

A helmet. And next to it, a body.

One that didn't appear to be breathing.

I jumped when I heard a hushed voice behind me. "I knew you'd come."

Chapter Two

I TURNED AROUND slowly.

The first thing I noticed was that the man wasn't as wide as he was tall, like King Ciaran. That was a relief.

He wore the armor of a soldier, but something told me that wasn't his true identity, just like it wasn't mine.

I unsheathed my sword and held it between us, keeping a safe distance from the stranger. "Who are you?"

"I think you know who I am," the figure replied. I could hear the smile in his voice. He lifted an unlit torch off the wall, and immediately, the end burst into flame. I recognized a pair of moss green eyes that stood out against a dark, horse-like face.

It was Rowan, the wizard that had given me my trial, the man who first said what my second form was.

I shifted backward and raised my blade higher. "What are you doing here?" The sorcerer hadn't given me a great impression the day I met him, and the fact that he had magic made me trust him even less.

He sauntered closer to the tip of the sword, green eyes glinting in the firelight. "I'm here to help. Your brother asked me to."

How did he know that Kurt and I were related? But I didn't dare ask the question aloud for fear of drawing out the conversation. "To help me save him?"

"Not exactly… And you won't find him in here."

I dug my nails into my palms. "Why not? Did you inform King Ciaran of my presence?"

He gave a short laugh. "No. The king knows that without me. One might call the ability a sixth sense. Usually, sorcerers feel inklings of power, depending on the strength of the host. Your power is some of the strongest I've traced, which makes you an easier target to catch. I can tell that you've grown a lot since we last met."

I swallowed hard. "Where is Kurt?"

He sighed. "Heavily guarded in the North Tower. Even with all your power, you won't be able to get through to him."

"If you're working with King Ciaran, then why haven't you attempted to arrest me?"

He scoffed. "Niko works for King Ciaran. Do you honestly think I would want to work alongside that pathetic maggot?"

I lowered the weapon slightly. "Why should I trust you?"

Rowan sighed. "Let me make this clear. Kurt knows about the new recruits that are being shipped in. Every day, the guards become more and more numerous and most have powerful abilities. It would take an entire army to free him now. That's why he doesn't want you to take the chance. That's why he sent me."

My heart fell as my mind raced through my options. "We could work together. Maybe we could get him out if we both…" I trailed off as he shook his head, a forlorn expression etched into his dark features.

"I've already dismissed the idea. There are many sorcerers here that are more powerful than me."

I jumped when someone rattled the doorknob and banged on the door, their armor clanging like a broken bell with each hit. "Open up! We know you're in there!"

I looked at Rowan with wide eyes. "What now?"

He stretched out his hand and a barely visible ripple of power sealed itself onto the door. He motioned for me to follow him. "That lock won't last for long. They just need another sorcerer to melt the magic away."

As I ran alongside him, I thought over his words. What he said about the growing numbers of guards was true. I'd seen that for myself.

We trailed through the dungeon quietly, alongside cells that were mostly empty. Had King Ciaran killed his prisoners or just poisoned their minds to serve him, like he'd done with Roland?

The passageway dipped down into a steep staircase that seemed to go on forever before we finally reached a fork that split into three separate tunnels. Rowan pointed to one directly ahead. "That should lead you outside," he said.

He turned back to face the way we'd come.

"What about you?" I asked.

"I'll make something up," he said with a sly smile. "Oh, and I almost forgot. Kurt wanted you to have this..." He reached into his pocket and pulled out a black gem hanging on a thin, gold chain. It looked a lot like the pendants worn during survival tests. How long ago that seemed... "It's a phantom stone," he added.

I took the necklace from his hand. "Why did he want me to have it? And what is a phantom stone?"

"You'll see," he answered. "Just don't put it on until you're a good distance away from here."

I studied his face for any sign of trickery, and while his expression appeared as impetuous as usual, I believed him to be sincere. I changed into half form and pocketed the gem, careful to avoid crushing the plant.

Rowan narrowed his eyes as he took in the scar that dragged its way up my neck. "Where did you get that?"

I considered whether or not to tell him, but decided to keep it to myself. "I got it in a challenge at the conservatory," I lied, my voice so steady that I almost believed myself. Hopefully, my face didn't give anything away.

Rowan sighed. "A shame the things they put those students through." Then, with a nod and one last cocky smile, he went back the way he came.

I didn't know whether to be angry or grateful toward him. He helped me escape, but couldn't we have at least *tried* to rescue Kurt? And did he really know the extent of my power?

But how could he? I didn't even know how powerful I was.

I left the Ginsian castle feeling hollow. Even if Kurt had sent Rowan to stop me, I still felt like a traitor. I was *right* there. In the *same* building. But I'd failed him.

And yet, somewhere deep inside, I trusted that Rowan was right. That the time for rescuing Kurt would come soon, but trying to free him now would have catastrophic results.

After finding my way back to the woods, I shifted form and took off toward the west, soon discovering some of the power behind the plant's strength. I had more speed and stamina than I knew what to do with. Just before I reached the ocean the next day, I only needed a few hours to rest before I was back up again and heading for Achron, where I hoped to run into Matilda and Burton, the people who'd been like family to Roland. They deserved to know everything that had happened on the Isle of Ginsey. I flew over shimmering ocean most of the day until I finally spotted the seahorse-shaped island from afar, just as the sun was beginning to set. Even I found it incredible that it had only taken two days to get from King's Crest all the way to Achron without tiring too much.

Once I reached the familiar city, I swooped down low—probably lower than I should have—eyes searching for the squat orange huts of the slums where Matilda and Burton lived. Because most of them looked the same, it was hard for me to remember which one was theirs. Luckily for me, Matilda was outside of hers, watering one of her many potted plants.

I landed nearby, startling her and a few nearby villagers before shifting into a human.

"Ivy!" she said, surprised. She looked around at her staring neighbors and set down her watering can. She hurried over and guided me toward her front door. "Why don't you come inside for a bit?"

I nodded and followed her into the house.

As soon as the door was shut behind us, she turned to me. "I thought you were trying to keep a low profile."

I rested my back against the door and shook my head. "So much has happened…it just doesn't matter to me as much as it did before."

She seemed to catch the dark tones in my voice because the next words out of her mouth were, "What's wrong?"

Despite my efforts to hold back the tears I'd kept in for so long, my emotions got the better of me. I wiped at my streaming eyes furiously and cleared my throat. "Roland...Roland is gone."

"Gone?" she said quietly. "As in…*dead*?"

I gave her miserable nod.

Matilda let her head drop into her hands, and after a moment, I watched as droplets of liquid splashed onto her dark blue dress. A sob escaped her. "Why must everyone I love die?"

Though I normally didn't comfort people through touch, I could tell we both needed it. I stepped forward and wrapped her in a hug. We stayed like that for a long time until our sobs finally died down.

"How did he go?" she finally asked.

"A poisonous dart," I answered. "But his death was not as sad as some. He accepted his fate and we got to say goodbye."

She looked up at the ceiling as she wiped away her tears. "At least there's that."

I smiled slightly. "I agree." I looked around the hut. "Where is Burton?"

Matilda drew in a trembling breath. "Out at sea, of course. I'll have to tell him when he gets back."

I swallowed more tears as I prepared to deliver the next batch of news. "There's something else that you need to know."

She took a deep breath. "What's that?"

"Jane is alive."

Her gaze jerked up to meet my own. "What? A-alive?"

I nodded. "I saw and spoke to her myself."

Matilda wiped away the last of her tears and turned away, but I could still see the hesitant smile on her lips. "My young Jane, still alive?" She turned back to me. "Is she doing well?"

I smiled faintly and nodded. "Yes. Very well. She's made a respectable life among the natives on the Isle of Ginsey. She's works as a healer." I didn't mention it was the natives that took Roland's life in the first place.

She choked out a laugh. "Jane always wanted to be an owl…" Her face became serious again. "But why hasn't she come back?"

"Ginsey and Pira are looking for her, and because she doesn't have a flyer's form, she doesn't think that she'll be able to get back to Leviatha."

She frowned. "I don't understand. What's she done to make Ginsey and Pira search for her?"

I shrugged. "We didn't get a chance to talk about that."

Matilda brought out a handkerchief and wiped her face with it and then began to busy herself in the kitchen. "Well…at least we know she's alive and safe." She glanced at me. "You must have traveled hard to be back here already. I know grief takes its toll on people," she trailed off and studied my face, before shaking her head and going to search through her pantry. "You must be hungry."

Just the mention of food made my stomach growl. I really wanted to get back on my journey, but I couldn't deny that the offer of a nice meal sounded like heaven to my ears.

She brought out a bowl and a spoon. "Luckily for you, I've already got some broth going." She ladled some out into the bowl and set it in front of me. "And of course, you must stay the night here."

"I'm afraid I can't," I said, pausing to blow on a spoonful of the steaming broth. "I need to get to the conservatory as soon as possible."

"But surely you need some rest..." she said, her eyebrows raised. "You look like death itself." She cut herself short on the last word, as if realizing it was inappropriate to say at the moment.

I gave her as reassuring a look as I could muster. "I'll be okay."

She studied me a while before shrugging. "If you're set on it, I won't stop you. Just know that if you ever need somewhere to stay, if you ever need someone to go to...you can always count on Burton and me."

I smiled at her. "Thank you, Matilda. That means a lot."

She sighed. "I only wish I could offer more."

"You've offered me what I've always dreamed of," I said wistfully. "A home and a family."

Chapter Three

THE MOON SHONE brightly as I sped toward the school. My anger grew with every mile that passed. When I finally spotted the dark buildings of the conservatory against the freshly falling snow, I was livid.

The headmaster was the reason for Roland's death. He was the one that sent us on the most dangerous quest possible. I angled my wings back and dove. There weren't any lights on in any of the buildings or tents. It was probably early morning, the time when almost everyone is asleep, but if I had to wait at Gibble's desk for the remainder of the night, I would.

I landed lightly on the ground and shifted into first form before making my way toward the boy's dorm. As I neared the doors, I noticed light shining through the cracks. Light that I hadn't seen before. Someone must be up after all.

I turned the handle and pushed the door open roughly only to be greeted by the sickening sight of the headmaster, fully dressed and beaming.

"Ivy! You've returned," he announced.

"How did you know I was here?" I questioned through gritted teeth. Just seeing his smiling face sent tremors of fury through my body.

"The sentinel spell I placed around the school, of course." His smile faded into a frown. "And speaking of the border, I can sense that you yourself have more power than when you left."

Another border spell? The fact that he was using magic similar to King Ciaran's set my teeth on edge. "If you mean that I've brought the plant with me, you'd be correct."

I changed into half-form and reached into my pocket, just brushing over glossy surface of Kurt's pendant before grabbing hold of the plant. I pulled it out. It was a lot more wilted than it had been the last time I'd seen it, but that was irrelevant to the plan that was already forming in my head.

The headmaster's eyes gleamed as he held out his hand. I didn't give it to him just yet. "Do you even wonder where Roland is?" I asked, the anger in my voice ringing through the air.

"Oh, yes...Where is Roland?" the headmaster asked. He glanced back at the plant before concentrating back on my face.

"Roland is dead, killed by the natives of the Isle of Ginsey."

The headmaster winced. "Well, that shows that even the best of the best can be conquered." He reached for the plant again, but I held it away.

"You told us that the plant would be easy to get to, but it was the most dangerous quest of all. You're the reason that Roland is dead," I accused.

He rolled his eyes. "Of course I'm not," he said gruffly. "The natives are. Now give me the plant."

"No," I replied firmly. As much as it hurt me to do what I was about to do, it needed to happen. I released my anger in the form of flames, and the plant disintegrated in my hand until it was just ash slipping through my fingers.

"No!" the headmaster shouted frantically. He tried to reach for the flower, but he'd reacted much too late.

He stared at my hand as I let the remaining ash fall to the ground. Slowly, dangerously, he looked back up at me with bared teeth. A deep, guttural sound escaped his throat. He glared as his skin began to shift. His canines enlarged and hair grew over his arms and legs. A plated armor vest replaced his usual black jacket.

He grabbed my wrist firmly, sharp nails digging into my skin, and dragged me down the corridor, away from his office. I would've been strong enough to pull away, but the power of his magic forced me forward.

When we reached a large wooden door, painted black, he unlocked it, swinging it open.

I peered down a flight of stone stairs, stumbling into the wall when Headmaster Drake jerked me down after him.

A dungeon? I'd had no idea that this was under the boy's dorms.

He opened one of the cells and flung me inside. My head slammed against the wall, and for a few seconds, everything went black. Blood dripped down my forehead and onto my neck, but the wound already prickled as it sealed itself closed.

"We'll see what a few days of no food or water will teach you," the headmaster growled. And with that, he slammed the cell door and stomped back up the stairs. The door squeaked as it shut, blanketing the room in darkness.

Behind me, I heard rustling in the hay, and I snapped my head around to look, expecting to see a rat. Instead, it was another person, a prisoner like me. In this darkness, there was no way to tell who it was.

"Hello?" I asked.

"Ivy?" replied a deep voice. "Is that you?"

"Grix!" I said in recognition.

The shadow stood up and gripped the bars in his hands. "You came back?"

"Of course!" I replied as I pushed myself to my feet. I shifted into half-form so I could see his face. "What happened to you? Why are you down here?"

His hooded eyes and sharper-than-usual cheekbones told me just how long he'd been down here.

Nevertheless, he barked out a laugh. "Because I took what you said seriously after you caught me bullying Alyss."

I remembered that girl. I remembered the fear in her eyes as she'd cowered behind her dark hair.

Grix continued on. "I knew that you were right. I'd been working for the headmaster, making sure that new students were put in their place. When you left, I decided to put an end to it, but the headmaster, as you can see, didn't like that plan." His smile morphed into a look of confusion as he asked, "Where's Roland? Why isn't he with you?"

I looked away. "He was killed."

Grix sat back down on the concrete slab—which was apparently a bed—and didn't speak for a long time. After a while, he whispered, "You wouldn't have thought someone like Roland was capable of dying."

I nodded and looked away, the lump in my throat threatening to choke away my breath.

Across from me, I heard a shift in the hay and spotted a small figure. My light didn't shine bright enough to see that far, but I could see the shadow of another prisoner.

"Hello?" I called over to them.

The figure stirred. "Hello," answered a small, female voice.

"That's Alyss," said Grix. "We were both brought here at the same time."

I narrowed my eyes. "Why?"

"I stood up to the headmaster when he imprisoned Grix," she said. "Right before he'd gone to talk to the headmaster, Grix had apologized and asked for my forgiveness."

"But let's get to the most important question," said Grix, seemingly trying to change the subject. "What are you doing here?"

"I completed my quest. I retrieved the plant of eternal life...but when I got here, I burned it to ashes in front of the headmaster," I explained.

Grix gave a laugh. "Whoa! Why'd you do that?"

"Mostly out of anger," I admitted. "And I don't believe anyone should live eternally. Especially not hi—"

I broke off when I heard scuttling nearby. I searched the floor and jumped away when a pile of straw close to my foot shifted and squeaked. "Was that a—?"

"Rat?" Alyss finished for me. "Yes."

I shuddered and climbed up onto the concrete slab to get farther away from the nasty creature.

"They get in your hair pretty often when you sleep," she remarked.

I peered closer as two beady eyes peeked up at me, hay framing the rodent's head like golden locks.

A hint of a smile played on my lips. "What if...that's really one of us? A shifter sent to rot down here?"

Grix cracked up. "Maybe it's Gibble."

I snorted. "So this is where he sleeps. I wonder where he stores all his papers."

Grix snatched up a piece of hay and peered at it closely. "I think I can see tiny letters."

Despite being cast into a prison of darkness and moldy hay and rats, we shared a laugh, even Alyss, who squeaked like a mouse herself.

The laughter faded off until everything was silent. After a while, I was pretty sure both of them had drifted off. I was too worried that a rodent would end up nesting on my head to think about sleep.

I waited for what felt like hours, curled up on the corner of the slab. Sometimes, I thought I could hear noises from the students above. They sounded more like traces of haunted memories.

I jolted when the door clattered open and the headmaster trotted down the steps, breathing hard and sweating profusely, no longer in his half-wolf form. The ring of keys he held chimed with every step, waking up both Alyss and Grix, if they'd been asleep in the first place.

I stood up, all thoughts of rodents forgotten.

He rattled a key in the lock to my chamber door as he hissed unintelligible words under his breath. It unlocked with a click. "Come on," he ordered, holding the door open.

My thoughts were in a muddle as I stepped out.

"Quickly," he said, pushing me forward. Before I knew it, we'd reached the steps and were climbing up. I looked back at Alyss and Grix's surprised faces, lit up by morning light that filtered in from upstairs, and then they were gone.

"What's this about?" I asked angrily as he set a fast pace toward the door that led outside. Was he going to punish me in front of all the students? And why was he being so panicked about it?

"We have company," he answered. "Important company."

He opened the door, and my questions fell silent as I took in the scene outside.

A large group of students and guards crowded around the road where I had been dropped off the day of my trial. The headmaster pushed past them, still forcing me to follow him.

I could see that the carriage was tall and made out of polished dark wood. Who could it be? Perhaps it was King Ciaran, here to claim me as his prisoner and to take me back to his dungeon to finish the ritual he'd started.

A tall man stood there, waiting to greet us. He held a helmet in one hand and rested his other hand on the hilt of his sword. His sandy blond hair was cropped close to his head, and boyish freckles dotted his nose in a way that only added to his handsomeness.

The headmaster moved out from in front of me. "Here is the girl you asked to see," he said with a bow.

I wasn't sure what to do, so I kept standing and studied the man with curiosity. He took me in for a second, his eyes squinting. Everything was quiet, as if even the horses were holding their breath. Then, his face spread into a smile.

He took his hand off his sword hilt and extended it to me. "Nice to finally meet you Miss Oliver. I am Prince Matthias."

My eyes widened and I dropped into a deep bow. "I'm sorry Your Highness. I did not realize you were royalty."

He pulled me up by my elbow. "You need not bow to me, Ivy. As far as I'm concerned, we're equals."

He held out his hand once again, and this time I shook it. "Thank you."

The prince turned and opened the carriage door, but paused to look back at me. "You can say goodbye to your friends before we leave."

Leave? "What? Where are we going?"

He raised an eyebrow. "Back to the castle. My father is looking forward to meeting you."

The king wanted to meet *me?*

He was about to turn back to the carriage, but I stumbled over myself to say, "Your Highness?"

The prince shook his head. "Please, just call me Prince Matthias, or even Matthias...but what is it?"

I glanced at the headmaster, who glared at me as if he'd already guessed what I was about to ask. "Could I take someone with me?"

The prince was silent for a moment as he thought, but eventually, he answered, "I suppose. You'll need someone to attend to you anyway."

I turned to the headmaster, suppressing a smile from my face. "Alyss and Grix would be perfect attendants," I prompted.

Headmaster Drake gritted his teeth, staring daggers at me.

Prince Matthias gave him a nod. "It looks like you'll be two students short."

The headmaster forced the corners of his mouth upward and gave a shallow bow before starting off toward the boys' dorm once again.

Finally, I had time to search the crowd of students for my friends. Liana stepped forward, as if knowing that I was looking for her. She looked tired and worn.

What had happened to her cheerfulness the month that I was gone? Perhaps she had heard the news about Roland, but I didn't think she knew Roland very well.

"How are things, Liana?" I asked quietly.

She looked down at the ground, and her mouth wavered. I instinctively reached out to hug her. She shook against my shoulder, but never made a sound.

I rubbed her back, awkwardly trying to comfort her, and waited for her to calm down enough to explain.

"I'm sorry, Ivy," she said after the shaking had abated. "Ever since you left things have gotten worse."

"How?" I asked.

She pulled away to look at my face. "My trainer disappeared. I don't know where he went...but January took his place."

"January? She's already a trainer?"

Liana nodded. "There aren't enough of them, so they had to replace them with Level Nines. Some of the students are even having to share trainers. Even Mrs. Scarls has vanished into thin air."

I frowned. "Last time I was here, there were so many that some of them had been appointed as guards instead."

"Not anymore."

I looked over at the prince. He was watching me, waiting patiently.

When I looked back at Liana, she seemed to have pulled herself back together. She gave me a nod. "Go. I'll be fine. I can deal with January. I'm a Level Eight now, so it won't be long before I can leave this place."

I glanced over the school grounds, before meeting her eyes again. "Be strong."

I saw a flicker of the old Liana when she smiled. "I will." Then, she sunk back into the crowd, just as Prince Matthias spoke up from behind me.

"Who was that girl?"

I jumped, unaware that he was that close. "Liana," I said as I turned to him.

"A good friend of yours, I'm guessing?" he questioned further.

"Yes."

I looked back at the boy's dorm just as Grix and Alyss came out of the building followed by Headmaster Drake. In the light, I could see just how dirty their clothes and faces were.

I watched as they made their way toward us. Then, something happened that I didn't expect. Natalia broke free of the throng of students. "Alyss!" she shouted.

Alyss turned around just before she was tackled with a hug.

I should have realized it before. They both had black hair, blue eyes, and the same pale complexion. They must be sisters.

Natalia kissed Alyss's forehead and said a few words. Alyss nodded, her mouth barely opening as she replied.

The headmaster took ahold of Alyss's arm, and Natalia stepped back as she was dragged away.

Roland had been Natalia's trainer. I needed to tell her about his death, in case she hadn't heard yet. I caught her gaze and lifted my hand in a wave.

She got the message and moved toward me through the crowd.

Before I could even speak up, she said, "You didn't come back with Roland. Where is he?"

This was something that I had dreaded from the time I left the island. As trainer and initiate, they must have been pretty close. After all, that was the person that they spent the most time with.

I found it hard to meet her eyes. "He isn't coming back," I said softly.

She closed her eyes and pursed her lips together, forming a thin line. I could tell that she was trying to hold back emotion. When she opened her eyes again, they were wet. She blinked several times. "How?" she demanded. Her voice cracked.

"A dart dipped in a sleeping draft. He was allergic to it," I answered.

I watched as her face morphed from melancholy to dangerous. "Natives," she hissed, her eyes unfocused. They centered on me after a few seconds. "And *you*. If you hadn't asked that he come with you, we would still have him."

I narrowed my eyes. "He used magic to get me to bring him along."

"You could have gone back to the headmaster and changed it," she snapped.

I crossed my arms. "How was I supposed to know that one of us would end up dead?"

She clenched her hands into fists without reply. She glared at me for a few more seconds before she swung around and walked off, ending our conversation.

Her words cut like a knife. I had always thought of us as friends, but now I felt like our friendship was severed. Maybe with time, it could be sewn back up.

I scanned over the crowd to see if I saw anyone else that I knew. There was Abby, standing on her tip-toes to see the prince. One of the boys that I'd been in a survival test with, talking to his friend. And in the back of the crowd, to the left, January.

She had on a different outfit than the students did, now that she was a trainer. She wore a black, formfitting suit and had her hair tied into a tight bun. She crossed her gloved hands over her chest and raised her eyebrows when she noticed me looking.

Whatever she had done to Liana in training, I hated her for it. She had taken away Liana's cheerful heart, and to me at that moment, it was an unforgivable crime. Liana had never been mean to her, not that I could remember. Liana was never mean to anybody.

I gave her a smoldering look, just as I felt a tap on my shoulder. I looked back to see the prince's anxious face. "We have to go, Ivy. It's a long journey, and we're pressed for time."

I searched for Liana once more to wave goodbye, but I didn't see her in the crowd anymore. "Your two friends are already mounted on their horses," the prince said as he led the way.

Prince Matthias helped me into the carriage, where I sat across from his guard, a man who kept a straight, emotionless face as he studied me silently. Then, once the prince was inside, the carriage surged forward.

I settled back in my seat in the uncomfortable silence that followed our departure.

Chapter Four

Every once in a while, Prince Matthias tried to make small talk, remarking on the weather and the upkeep of the conservatory, but I barely contributed. Instead, my mind focused on the days ahead. Would I finally be able to study this prophecy that so many people had talked about? And should I even believe it when I did?

I glanced over at the guard, who still hadn't said a word. His hair was a dark chestnut color and despite the constant line between his brows, his eyes were a soft brown. They reminded me of Roland.

Everything around me seemed to fade as I recalled Roland's easy-going laugh and his friendliness toward others.

I remembered the time when we saw the fire-dancers, when he'd tried to comfort me after I got trampled by the crowd. I shouldn't have made such a big deal out of it. He was just trying to show me what Achron was famous for, and it was wonderful...until the tent caught on fire.

I remembered how he had kept me from going overboard on Burton's ship and made sure I was safe. I remembered floating down the canal in Nalla and laughing together as a Nallan man put flowers over Kurt's head... And the time just before his mind was invaded, when he'd shown me his half-form. If the moment had lasted a little longer...

And then I remembered his last message to his family. *I've seen what is to come in the next life. Do you honestly think that I would want to live in this world forever? Ivy, for those who believe, there is no death. Instead, there is a door to forever. A forever without anguish, without worry, without fear. And I am going to live in that forever.*

When I came back to the real world, the prince was watching me with a frown. I must look foolish, staring blankly at the carriage wall. I quickly looked outside. We sat silently for a while as the carriage descended the mountain, rocking us back and forth with the horses' gait.

What does the castle look like? Having started life as the lowest of the low, on the farthest island, the prospect hadn't even crossed my mind. Any news we got about the royal family, which wasn't much, was like hearing a bedtime story. Marvelous tales of evening dances, visiting princesses, and beautiful weddings. One of the first stories I'd heard of the royal family was the tragic passing of the queen after she'd delivered the twin princes. That had occurred years before I was born. And now, I was sitting beside one of the boys, our knees occasionally brushing when the carriage sprang over a bump in the road.

And what is the king like? Kurt had told me that King Giddon had bought him back from King Ciaran once. Did I dare have such high hopes that he would do it again? But now, I doubted King Ciaran would take any sum of money to release him, knowing that he was the strongest link to my cooperation if he ever managed to capture me.

The prince let out a deep breath of air. I hated to be such a boring audience, so I tried to come up with something to say. "How long will it take to get to the castle, Your Highness?" I asked.

Prince Matthias glanced at me. "About six days, give or take. It depends on the weather." He paused and smiled. "And I told you not to call me that."

I blushed and ducked my head. "Sorry."

He waved off my apology.

"Where will we be stopping?" I asked.

"We'll probably make a camp before we get to the sea."

I nodded and silence followed.

Then, "How has your time at the conservatory been?" Matthias's gray eyes were dark with curiosity.

I don't even know anymore... After a few long seconds, I decided to say, "Not too hard, now that I look back on it."

"Is that where you got that scar?" he asked, gesturing to my shoulder.

No matter how much I hated to bring up the subject, I didn't feel like I could lie to the prince.

"No, actually," I said as I pulled my sleeve back into place to cover the marred flesh.

His eyebrows furrowed. "Oh. May I ask how?"

I bit my lip. *I'd better tell him the truth.* "Have you heard of the plant of eternal life?"

The guard suddenly took interest in our conversation, studying me with knitted eyebrows.

The prince gestured to him. "Sir Lochlan here has always had quite an interest in the plant. And the Isle of Ginsey specifically. I know the island is real, but I always thought the plant was a myth."

Sir Lochlan turned away, but I knew he was still listening.

"It is most certainly real," I said, resisting the urge to trace over the scars with my fingertips.

"So...you're telling me...that you consumed the plant?" the prince concluded.

"Only a little made it into my system, so I don't think it will affect me the same way. But it did give me this scar."

"Hmm," said the prince, studying it. "It's strange. If the plant is supposed to make you stronger, then why is it hurting you?"

My stomach tightened as my mind worked around that question. Why *was* it hurting me? "I don't know," I said softly.

There was no more conversation after that. Everyone was wrapped up in their own thoughts as the carriage kept rocking back and forth.

We stopped before dark, where the smell of the ocean was strong. We had to be close.

While the camp was being built, I decided to stretch my legs with a walk through the woods. I followed the sound of trickling water until I came across a stream.

I stooped to drink, cupping my hand in the cold water to bring it to my mouth, but froze when I heard the snap of a twig. In the reflection of the stream, I could make out a dark, cloaked figure standing too close for comfort.

Time slowed. In a flash, I turned and grabbed the hooded figure's wrist, twisting it behind their back until I heard a cry of pain.

"Who are you?" I hissed.

"P-please, Ivy. It's me!"

I knew that voice.

My scowl disappeared and the tension seeped from my body. As soon as I let go of his arm, he flipped his hood back.

"Ayon?" I asked as I met his blue eyes.

He clutched his arm where I had grabbed him. "Yes," he said, his eyes pained.

My heart sunk. "I'm so sorry," I said, folding back his sleeve to look at the damage that I'd done. There were spots of blue already.

He jerked his arm away from my grasp.

I narrowed my eyes. "Why did you sneak up on me?"

He sighed and let his arm drop to his side. "I just wanted to surprise you."

"Well, you succeeded. What are you doing here, Ayon?"

He stiffened at my tone. "When I heard that the prince was at the conservatory, I made the trip out there just to find out he'd already left, and the phoenix was with him. You see, I've been wanting to get a job at the castle, and since the prince has showed interest in you...I wondered if you might help me out?" His mustered up a small smile. "Plus, I couldn't pass up the chance to see you again."

I scrutinized him, remembering very well that the last time we'd seen each other, he'd asked me to marry him.

Before I could reply, Ayon went on to say, "I plan to bring my fiancée to the castle to find work as well, but I wanted to make sure that there was a chance there for both of us before we committed to it."

Any suspicions I had were immediately erased. "Fiancée? Who?"

Ayon held his head higher. "Emillia Lisborne."

I knew Emillia, although I'd never talked with her very much. From what I could tell, she was a quiet, sweet girl that deserved Ayon's attention. She'd been an orphan, like myself, and had gone through her trial before me. Her second form, a sparrow, suited her personality perfectly.

I was surprised to feel a pang of jealousy. *It only took him a few months to get over me?*

I forced my mouth into a smile. "That's...great. Emillia is a wonderful girl."

Ayon nodded. "Yes, she is."

It's for the best. Perhaps now, we could be friends again.

"How is Elna doing?" I asked.

"She's been good. She still can't cook, though." The thought of Elna's cooking brought a grin to my face. Although life was easier back then, her food was the one thing that I didn't miss. Ayon continued. "She has to keep herself from telling everyone what happened in the arena, it was such a spectacle."

My smile faded. If she told anyone under seventeen what had occurred, she could be in danger of imprisonment. I usually remembered her endless chatter fondly, but now, I could only feel dread.

Ayon interpreted my expression. "Don't worry, we've both kept silent for the most part."

Relieved, I let my face relax. I looked behind Ayon, where I could barely see the tents still being set up through the trees. "Would you like to meet the prince?" I asked, focusing on him again.

"That's why I'm here. Will that be okay with him?" he asked.

"I'm pretty sure it will," I said as I started forward.

Ayon nervously followed me, a hand running through his hair.

When I came back into the sight of one of the guards, he nodded, acknowledging my presence, but froze when he saw Ayon.

"He's a friend," I reassured him.

The guard relaxed somewhat, but kept his hand near his sword hilt.

Sir Lochlan turned at the sound of our voices. He looked at Ayon and then back at me with a question in his eyes.

"Sir Lochlan, this is Ayon. He's an old friend of mine," I said as we approached.

Ayon stuck out a hand. Sir Lochlan looked at it for a moment before he finally consented to shake it.

I smiled nervously. "He is headed to the castle looking for work."

Sir Lochlan frowned. "What's your form?"

"A horse, so a stable-hand is what I had in mind," Ayon answered.

"We have enough stable-hands already."

I opened my mouth to protest, but Sir Lochlan continued on. "—we are, however, in need of trainers. Not many people are willing to risk their lives to tame wild horses."

Ayon's eyes widened. If I wasn't mistaken, being a trainer was a step up, even if it was dangerous.

"Of course, the prince has more say in this matter. I'll go ask him for you."

I watched as Ayon's Adam's apple bobbed up and down nervously.

"Don't worry. He doesn't bite. An execution, however..." Sir Lochlan trailed off. He smiled and continued on into the prince's tent.

Ayon looked at me, worried. "Are you sure it'll be okay to ask him?"

I rolled my eyes. "Sir Lochlan is messing with your mind. Prince Matthias isn't that kind of person." Of course, I'd only known him for less than a day, so I couldn't be completely confident in that statement.

Then, the prince's tent flap opened again and Prince Matthias stepped out. "I'm glad to hear that you think so."

"Y-your Highness!" Ayon stuttered, falling to one knee in a bow.

"Please, rise. What is your request?" said the prince patiently.

"Uh…well, I was wondering if I could get a job at the castle…Your Highness," Ayon said, brow furrowed as he struggled to get back up.

"Hmm," Prince Matthias hummed. He glanced at me for a moment before looking back at Ayon. "What kind of job?"

"A stable-hand or a horse trainer," Ayon answered, regaining some of his courage.

"Have you had any experience with either?"

"I've been a stable-hand for the past two and a half years," Ayon confirmed.

"But no experience with training, I take it?"

Ayon shook his head.

"He's a good worker," I spoke up. "When I used to visit him, he rarely took breaks."

The prince studied Ayon. "Well, perhaps you could start out as a stable-hand while the Horsemaster trains you how to break an untamed horse."

Ayon's shoulders relaxed as he nodded. "That sounds like a generous offer, Sir." He shot me a grateful look.

Prince Matthias shifted his feet. "Will you be traveling with us?" he asked. "I'm afraid we don't have any horses to spare, but since you are one…" He trailed off.

Ayon shook his head. "No, sir. I have a wedding in two weeks' time."

"I take it your fiancée will need a job as well, then?" questioned the prince.

"I wouldn't want to ask too much," Ayon said cautiously.

"Nonsense," the prince replied. "What is her second form?"

"A sparrow, Your Highness."

The prince crossed his arms. "So she could be a maid. The castle is always in need of another maid. You'll have your work cut out for you by the time you reach the castle, I guarantee it."

"Thank you so much, Your Grace," Ayon said with a bow.

Prince Matthias patted him on the shoulder. "Consider it a wedding present." Then, he ducked back into his tent.

"Thank you, Ivy," said Ayon as we walked toward the woods again. "If you weren't here, I don't think I'd have the courage to approach the camp."

His praise felt odd. It was usually him that dove headfirst into situations, him that had any connections with the outside world.

Ayon's expression saddened as if he had read my thoughts. "You really are different, you know?" he said.

"It's been tough," I admitted.

"Maybe we can talk about it when I get to the castle."

"Assuming I'll still be there when you arrive," I said solemnly.

"Why wouldn't you be?" he asked.

I shrugged. "Two weeks is a long time, that's all."

We stopped walking just before we got to the tree line.

Before he continued into the woods, he pulled me into a hug. "It's good to finally see you again," he said.

I nodded against his shoulder uncomfortably. He was almost a married man. I wasn't sure if we should be treating each other like we used to.

I watched his retreating back until the trees swallowed him completely, remembering a time when he had been my best friend. It was nice while it lasted, but now we were older and going our separate ways. Perhaps when he moved to the castle, Emillia and I could be good friends, but things could never be the same with Ayon.

After I turned away from the woods, Sir Lochlan waved me over to where he stood, in front of the second largest tent. "This will be where you sleep for the night," he explained. "Two guards will be stationed outside at all times—," he said gruffly before I cut him off.

"Don't waste the guards. I don't need them," I said.

"There are bandits in this part of the forest. The prince just wants to ensure your safety."

"I can protect myself," I protested, crossing my arms.

"He insisted," Sir Lochlan said. "And as his subject, you will comply."

I sighed. "Fine."

Sir Lochlan gave a sharp nod and turned away. "Good."

Chapter Five

THAT NIGHT, AS we sat around the campfire to eat dinner, my thoughts returned to the pendant that Rowan passed on from Kurt. Unfortunately, I could only get to it in half form, so I'd just have to wait until everyone else went to bed.

Alyss and Grix approached me as I tore into the leg of a rabbit the guards had caught and roasted on a spit. I probably looked like a barbarian, but my hunger took me past caring. They shot worried glances at the intimidating Sir Lochlan, who sat between me and the prince, the two people he needed to protect the most. He'd eaten quickly, and was now glowering at them as he sharpened a knife, as if considering whether or not they were a threat.

Grix spoke up first. "We just wanted to say thank you, Ivy. It was a relief to finally see the light of day."

"And I've always wanted to go to the castle," said Alyss quietly.

I took the time to swallow before answering. "Think nothing of it. It's nice to have someone I know on this journey."

Alyss smiled timidly. "You don't know me very well yet, but I hope that we can be friends by the end of this trip."

"I'm sure we will," I said with a slight smile as I raised a canteen to my lips.

Later that evening, I was restless. I wanted to study Kurt's pendant, but I was certain that the glow of my skin would attract attention through the thin canvas walls. I was beginning to dislike the fact that I could only get to it in half-form.

Outside, the guards talked quietly to keep themselves awake, but it kept me awake, too. Finally, when their voices died down for a few minutes, my eyes drifted closed, but no matter how much I willed myself to sleep, I simply couldn't.

It felt like hours before I heard the snores outside the tent. I sat upright and tossed aside the covers, quietly lifting the tent flap to find both guards sleeping as soundly as babes. I grinned at my luck, and tiptoed outside. Two more guards were stationed near the fire, right outside the prince's tent. I crouched behind a fallen log before they could spot me. They didn't notice a thing.

With silent, bare feet on the cold grass, I hurried deeper into the woods, trying to avoid twigs and rocks. When I was sure that I was too far away for anyone to see the swirls of light, I changed into my half-form body, heightening my already strong senses. I was rocked backward by the power that enveloped me. I'd felt nothing like it before, but it worried me. Just how much would this plant change me before it finally settled down?

Worried that the guards in the camp would be able to see me after all, I traveled even deeper into the forest. I pulled the phantom stone out of my pocket and studied it as I walked, turning it in my fingers. There was no inscription carved into it, nothing that differentiated it from any other survival test necklace. I slipped it over my head...

And my vision went dark. A dizzying sensation shivered through my body, and I suddenly felt as if the sky had swallowed me whole and spat me back out again.

Suddenly, I was in a dark room that smelled of rot and mold, staring at a figure hunched in the corner. I knew my heart should be beating hard in my chest, but the strange thing was, I couldn't feel it. There was no glow from my limbs either, because my entire body had turned into a translucent grayish blue.

I tried to speak. "Hello?" I said to the figure in the corner.

The figure flinched and turned its head in my direction. He didn't have time to say anything before something clanged loudly. I pushed myself into a corner as a heavyset guard walked by, lantern in one hand and the other pulling along a cart of limp, bloodied bodies.

Light flashed over the room we were in as the man held the lantern up to the bars. "Still alive, eh?" he grunted with a scowl, his breath puffing out in a white cloud. "I guess the king would be mad if you weren't."

The face of the prisoner was lit up for just a few seconds, but it was enough for me to recognize the drawn face and dull green eyes. It was my brother, but an emptier version of him.

As the man rolled the cart away, I whispered, "Kurt, it's Ivy."

"I know," he said, his voice cracking as he watched the light of the lantern creep farther away.

"How is this working?" I asked.

He leaned forward and crawled to the stone slab in the corner, digging under it to pull out a matching black gem. "Rowan made them," he said in a rusty voice. "They're connected together somehow. Whenever one is slipped on, it takes that person wherever the other pendant is." He coughed, and pulled his ragged clothes tighter around him. It must've been cold here, but I couldn't feel anything.

"What have they done to you?" If I were in my normal body, tears would spring to my eyes, but in this strange spirit body, there weren't any.

"They want to keep me alive, but barely," he rasped. "Every day they take me to the room with dark red walls. It reeks of death and rot and the heat from the torches only makes it worse. They want me to tell them about you. Your weaknesses, your strengths, your location, anything... But I won't," he breathed. "No matter how much of my blood they use to paint those dark red walls."

If I were in my normal body, I would've felt sick. I struggled to find the words to speak.

Kurt was hurting for me. Hurting so that they wouldn't know where I was. "You have to tell them. If you died..." I didn't finish the sentence. He knew what would happen if he died. "I can't have you die, too. Not after Roland. Not after Mother and Father."

"Roland's dead?" he said flatly.

"Yes... And he wasn't who you thought he was," I added quickly. "Something was controlling him, making him do all those awful things."

"I'd hoped so," he replied. "As soon as you broke the spell, it was obvious that he didn't know what was happening...which is why I didn't toss him off my back when we were trying to escape."

I looked down as I remembered that day. "Before he died, I tried to save him. Tried to give him the plant of eternal life, but he wouldn't take it."

He raised his eyebrows, the first flicker of hope settling over his features. "You got to the plant?"

I nodded. "I did. And some of it got into my system when I accidentally punctured the stem."

He sat up straighter. "So you're telling me...you're immortal."

I shook my head. "I heal quickly and I'm stronger, but...I'm not sure if I'm immortal. I didn't consume the whole thing."

He shrugged, and then winced as if he'd hurt something. "Stronger is good. It will help you with your destiny...whatever that may be."

"Can't it help me rescue you? I was right there, in the same building, and Rowan turned me away."

"No. No, if you get caught, it'll put you and the rest of the world in danger," he said.

I tilted my head. "The rest of the world?"

"Don't you realize why King Ciaran wants you? He wants your power. To control you and use you against his enemies."

I went quiet, and eventually, Kurt broke the silence. "If I tell them things about you Ivy, they'll only kill me sooner. Once they have enough information about you, I'll be useless and they'll either stop bringing me food or kill me on the spot."

"As long as I'm alive, they'll consider you the bait to get to me," I said softly. "But you need to tell them something, if only to keep from being tortured."

He didn't reply. "Ivy, there's something that you have to know," he finally said. "Mother...is dead."

I knitted my eyebrows. "I know. I just said that a moment ago."

He sighed. "Well...Father isn't dead."

"What do you mean?" I asked. "How is that possible?"

He leaned back into the wall, as though bracing himself for the next words. "He's working for King Ciaran."

I wished my body could feel something. The cold that didn't bite, the tears that didn't fall, the heartbeat that was absent. But there was nothing.

Should I be angry or sad or relieved?

"How—how did you come to know this?" I forced out.

Kurt's breath puffed out in white fog as he whispered, "He's the painter."

Chapter Six

Before I could reply, the sky sucked me up again and plunged me back down into my body with a jolt that sent my heart hammering as if it had just remembered how to beat. Kurt's expression as he said those last few words seemed to linger in the silhouette of trees overhead. I blinked once in confusion, but it took only a few seconds to discover why I'd returned to my body.

"What 'ave we got 'ere? I thought fer certain you were dead."

I jerked my head slightly and caught sight of a man above me. He grinned from ear to ear beneath a speckled gray beard, his eyes shimmery black pools of malevolence. In his rough, dirt-stained fingers, he held the phantom stone. I sat up quickly, leaves falling from my tangled hair, reaching for the sword that was no longer at my side.

One by one, men sauntered out of the shadows and joined their leader, eyeing their newest find. The leader swung the pendant from side to side.

"It couldn' be black diamond, could it?" he asked with a twisted smile.

I pushed myself to my feet slowly, calmly. "I'm not looking for trouble."

"Doesn't look like it to me," snickered one of the men behind me. "Laying down on the ground with your skin glowing like that."

I turned to face the man that had spoken.

"Got anything else valuable?" he asked. He stalked around me like a cat, eyeing me up and down.

My muscles tensed. "I'm not your prey," I snarled.

He sneered and looked over his shoulder. "What do you say we take her to camp, boys?"

Their faces glowed as they shouted in agreement.

Someone shoved me forward from behind, and the man caught me, digging the hilt of his blade into my back. "Then let's go!" he barked as he tried to push me forward.

That was enough to send me over the edge. In an explosion of rage, I whirled on him and hooked his jaw so forcefully that it cracked. He fell to the ground, suddenly still. I reached down and took his knife while the other men stared at their fallen comrade in shock, the grins wiped from their faces.

Taking advantage of their shock, I kicked the feet out from under the leader and pried the phantom stone out of his grasp. He was stunned to find himself on his back, gasping for the air I'd knocked out of his lungs. Before he had a chance to react, I'd already swiped the gem and pocketed it.

Realizing what I'd done, he grabbed my ankle, digging in with his short, stubby nails. "I want that diamond!" he shrieked, spit flying from his mouth.

With a simultaneous roar, the other bandits rushed at me, their weapons raised. The nearest one carried my sword. I dodged his badly aimed swipe and slashed at the hand that held it. He moved faster than I'd expected.

Instead of me wounding him, he managed to slash through the leather of my glove and deep into my flesh. I hissed through my teeth, trying not to focus on the pain as I used the man's moment of victory against him. I twisted the hilt out of his hand into mine, and when I hit his temple, he dropped like a fly.

I started to turn toward the others, but before I could face them fully, something sharp plunged into my back. I cried out, faltering momentarily.

The bandits didn't hesitate once I was weakened. One punched me in the nose while another kicked me to the ground. Blood seeped out of my mouth, but the kicks kept coming until black spots clouded my vision.

"NO!" came a sudden, furious shout. There was a click and the whistle of an arrow before it embedded itself in flesh with a thud. A howl sounded, and one of the bandits fell to the ground next to me. His body twisted away at an odd angle so that I could see the thick arrow shaft sticking out of his back.

There were more running footsteps and then the sound of ringing steel. Most of the bandits knew to run away, shifting into various forms—a squirrel, a warthog, a cat—but one bandit foolishly tried to get the pendant out of my hand.

Not a second after he touched me, there was a click, a whistle, and a thud. The bandit landed heavily beside me, his face buried in the leaves and mud, one eye staring blankly.

"Ivy!" said Prince Matthias' voice, rushing toward me and brushing the hair out of my eyes. I stared at his blurry figure, unable to breath.

"Lochlan, come here!"

Another figure appeared from the other side and rolled me over. I winced and tried to suck in a breath of air, but was only met with a stabbing pain.

"She's badly wounded. See the way the blood foams? Punctured lung, I think," said Sir Lochlan.

"What do we need to do?" Matthias asked.

Sir Lochlan hesitated. "Hold on. Look." He pulled off the glove that had been cut through with a sword. Slowly, my vision started to clear. The prince and Sir Lochlan both stared at my hand as the flesh grew back over it.

At the same time, my broken nose snapped back into place, bringing tears to my eyes.

Sir Lochlan narrowed his eyes in disbelief. "Hold her down tight," he said to Prince Matthias.

He grabbed the knife in my back and yanked it out. I jerked violently and sent the prince sprawling.

I rolled onto my hands and knees as I coughed up blood. It became easier to breathe as my lung healed itself. My broken and bruised ribs slowly began to mend. I wiped my face on my glove and tried to stand. Sir Lochlan helped me up while the prince stood and watched in fascination as the fresh, blue bruises that lined my arms and face faded.

"What is this?" he asked in a hushed voice.

"It's the plant," I replied weakly.

"It healed her," Sir Lochlan said.

My entire body shook with fatigue as I took a step forward. "We should get back to camp."

"This way," said the prince, taking me by the arm and turning us to the right. The few times that I accidentally tripped, he made sure that I didn't fall.

Sir Lochlan watched for any other threats, not even bothering to sheath his bloodied sword. Every now and then he would make us stop to listen, but there was nothing.

The sky lightened as dawn crested over the horizon. When we could finally see the glow from the dying campfires, enough of my strength had returned that I managed to walk by myself. The guards were busying themselves around the site, patrolling, packing up, and cooking breakfast. As we neared, the ones who noticed us eyed my shredded clothing and Lochlan's sword. "Everything all right?" the closest guard called.

"Bandits," Sir Lochlan said darkly. "It's settled now."

The flap of a nearby tent opened and Grix peered out, a pillow mark still lined on his face. "Bandits? Did they hurt anyone?"

"Do any of us look hurt?" Sir Lochlan barked as he sulked away.

I raised my eyebrows at Lochlan's tone, and Grix, looking affronted, ducked back inside without answering.

The prince placed his hand on my elbow and led me to my tent. "See if you can get some rest. We'll be leaving within the hour."

I nodded and slipped inside, dropping onto the mat. Even though I was exhausted, I could only listen to the activity of the camp. It felt like only a few minutes had passed before Alyss shook my shoulder.

The guards deconstructed my tent quickly. Once it was packed with the other things on the top of the carriage, the prince climbed inside. Sir Lochlan turned back to me, his hand held out to help me inside, but was greeted with a gust of wind in the face as I took off into the sky in phoenix form. I circled over them, ready to get going.

Lochlan raised his hand to the sky and shouted, "Seriously?"

The prince poked his head out and looked up. He muttered something, and Sir Lochlan gave up on me and pulled himself into the carriage, shutting the door behind him.

Relieved that I would be allowed to stay this way, I looked forward. At my height, the ocean was already visible, a blue line that stretched across the horizon as far as the eye could see. Below, the trees and grass gave way to rocks and sand. I closed my eyes as the cold wind rippled through my feathers. My thoughts were clearer in the sky.

The moment of peace couldn't last long. Before I knew it, Kurt's words about our father rushed back into my mind. *He's the painter.* He was the person that smeared the blood of prisoners over the walls of the torture chamber. His own son's blood.

I hoped that Kurt was wrong, that the painter just looked like our father. Better to have a dead father who lived an honest life than a living father who abandoned his children to work for King Ciaran.

We traveled for about two hours before I was forced to land. The carriage and horses had stopped at the docks, just past a small village.

The ship was a good size, big enough to hold all of us and our horses. Almost everyone, including Alyss and Grix, went below decks for rest after the early start they'd had. I wanted to sleep, wanted to let it take my troubles away for even the smallest moment, but my mind was still reeling from this morning's events. Instead, I sat on a barrel and watched the land fade in the distance. It was just a small, dark hill on the horizon when a shadow fell over me. I looked up at Sir Lochlan.

"Can I ask you something?" His eyes dared me to say no.

"Of course," I answered.

"When you went on the quest for the plant, did anyone...go with you?" He clenched his jaw as he waited for me to reply.

I looked away. "Yes."

"Where are they now?" he asked.

I glanced up at him, confused as to why he was interested in asking. "One of them, my brother, is in King Ciaran's dungeon, and the other—" I couldn't meet his gaze. "The other one died. An allergic reaction to the natives' sleeping draft."

Sir Lochlan's voice was barely above a whisper when he asked, "What was his name?"

"Roland," I answered quietly.

There was no reply, but Sir Lochlan's shadow stayed where it was. I looked up at him, and was utterly surprised to see that his eyes were red and watery. He dashed the tears away with the back of his hand, and turned to the ocean so that I wouldn't be able to see his emotion.

"Roland…Roland was my brother," he choked out.

Chapter Seven

I GOT TO my feet and backed away, struggling to find words.

Sir Lochlan continued. "He wrote me a letter, telling me that he was going on a quest to the Isle of Ginsey. I already knew of his condition, of course."

"His condition?" I rasped.

"The dark magic that had been planted in his mind by King Ciaran."

I stared at his ashen face. "You knew about that?"

"I was the only one he ever told. And luckily, I'd heard of a way to cure him. At least, I thought it was luck at the time. I didn't know that the natives would kill him." After a few seconds, he turned back to me, his normally emotionless eyes glistening with unshed tears. "We'll be passing through my hometown. My parents and siblings deserve to know what happened."

I looked up at the white sails, finding it hard to meet his eyes. "Before Roland died, he asked me to pass a message on to his family—that he'd seen what was to come after life and that he's in a place without pain or fear."

Sir Lochlan formed his lips into a hard line. "He was wrong. There is no afterlife."

I studied him. "Where do you think we go when we die?"

"We just...end. There is nothing more. There is no *after*."

I shook my head. "I can't believe that. Not after all that I've seen."

"What have you seen?"

I sat back on my hands. "When I went to retrieve the plant, there were four trials that I had to undergo," I recalled. "In the last, I was in a spiritual realm where angels were fighting demons. When a demon tried to attack me, the most powerful angel protected me and tested my heart to see if I was worthy to continue to the plant."

"Which you obviously were," Sir Lochlan said. "But that doesn't prove anything. It was probably an illusion, like the trials we go through for our second forms or the survival tests that Roland talked about."

"No, this was different," I said. "I was able to take the plant, and you can't take anything out of an illusion."

He crossed his arms. "You can't persuade me, and Roland couldn't either. He's already tried."

I pressed my lips closed, irritation choking out my thoughts like dark vines. I slid down from the barrel, but before I turned, Sir Lochlan spoke up. "You can still tell my family what Roland wanted you to say when we reach Redrune tomorrow. You should just know that they probably won't take it too well, either."

Tomorrow? So soon? I struggled to keep the bitterness out of my voice as I replied, "Thanks for the warning."

I walked to the hatch and stepped down the ladder into the darkness below, mind spinning.

All the cots were occupied by guards, most of whom were snoring loudly. Alyss and Grix sat across the room on crates, talking quietly. They looked up as I came down the steps.

I must not have hid my emotion very well because Grix asked, "What's wrong?"

"Oh, nothing. Just a discussion with Sir Lochlan," I said, trying to keep my voice nonchalant.

"Seems more like you had an argument," said Grix.

I shrugged. "You can hardly talk to Sir Lochlan without a fight. Anyway, how has your journey been?" I asked, changing the subject.

Alyss glanced up. "I'm not really used to riding horseback."

"That's an understatement," Grix added, stretching out his legs slowly, his face scrunched in pain. "We can barely move."

I blushed, embarrassed that I hadn't thought of their comfort before now. "I'll ask the prince if you can ride in the carriage next time."

"Please don't," said Alyss. "I don't want to be a burden."

I almost laughed. "You aren't a burden. And it might give me more chances to fly."

She looked away, a crease forming between her brows. "I hope you're right."

Grix slid his legs back and shifted forward on the crate, curiosity sparking in his eyes. "By the sound of it, you didn't get too much sleep last night. What did the bandits do to you?"

"Well, they were trying to steal my pendant and my sword. I couldn't leave without my things…so I took a beating."

"You had to fight them?" Alyss squeaked. She studied my arms and legs. "I don't see any marks."

"They healed before I got to camp. Without the plant, I would've died."

"The plant?" Alyss said, her head tilting to the side.

My mouth hung open wordlessly. I'd forgotten that I hadn't told them how the plant had affected me.

Grix sat up straight, eyes wide. "The plant of eternal life? You told me you'd burned it in front of the headmaster."

There was no turning back now. "I-I consumed it by accident on the way here…but not all of it. So I don't think I'm completely immortal."

"How did it happen?" Alyss questioned.

Reluctantly, I dove into the story, explaining how the serum had gotten into my system and made its mark on my shoulder, and how it affected me physically in the fight afterward. I left out the part about killing the man. It wasn't something I was proud of.

Alyss and Grix listened without interrupting, and when I'd finished, they sat for a while longer, speechless. At last, Grix shook his head. "To think I thought I could beat you on your first day at the conservatory. And now you're the most powerful creature in the world."

I snorted. "I'm not the most powerful."

"Then who is?" Alyss asked, thin eyebrows raised. "Who else has a trace of immortality in their blood?"

"There are sorcerers out there who can do some pretty powerful things. Healing themselves could be one of them," I said.

Grix let out a long whistle. "One thing is for sure—those bandits chose the wrong girl to mess with."

"To tell the truth, I don't know what would've happened if the prince and Sir Lochlan hadn't shown up when they did," I confessed.

I looked toward the cots when a guard snored loudly, then decided to change the subject. "How long do you think it'll be before the guards let one of us sleep?"

"Some of them have shifts coming up above decks. We're close to pirate waters, after all," Grix said.

Alyss whipped her head toward him. "We are?"

Grix gave her a reassuring half smile. "I don't think they'll attack us. When they notice the royal crest, they'll know that they're no match for our trained fighters."

"Or they'll just think we have more valuables," she mumbled.

Grix's smile slipped. "Or that."

"Do you know how long it will be before we reach the shore?" I asked.

"I think I heard someone say it would take six hours," Grix said.

I sighed in relief. "Good. I'm starting to feel the effects of a sleepless night."

Luckily, only an hour passed before some of the guards started to pry themselves from the cots and armor back up. I'd begun to doze off, so when Alyss and Grix insisted that I take the first cot available, I was grateful.

How will I tell Roland's family what happened? I thought as I drifted off. *What can I say that would soften the blow?*

I slept as much as I could before we had to get off the ship at around noon. When we docked, I made sure that Alyss and Grix got their turn in the carriage and promptly took off into the air afterward. We camped in a field that night, and though I wanted to put the pendant back on to check in on Kurt, there wasn't one moment that the prince didn't have someone watching me, whether it be Sir Lochlan, Grix, Alyss, or one of the other guards. I decided it would have to wait for the next day, perhaps after Sir Lochlan and I visited his family.

The next day was much the same, although the trees grew fewer, replaced by rocks and cliffs and the greenest of grass. The sight was spectacular from my vantage point in the clouds.

And then my eyes clapped upon Redrune and my flight faltered.

Statues that were carved into the mountain surrounded the city. Each one, dressed in heavy battle armor, stretched high up into the clouds, their heads barely visible through the mist. I swooped downward to get a closer look when I noticed that the road snaked up a hill to go right through the mouth of one beheaded statue. I shivered.

A shrill whistle sounded from below. The carriage had stopped and Sir Lochlan was waving me down. I dove and shifted form after landing.

Before I was fully restored to first form, Sir Lochlan was already lecturing me. "We're going through the tunnel, and the prince and I agree that you will be a lot safer in the carriage than in the sky. There could be spies in the big city."

"Okay," I said. "But I could just ride one of the spare horses." I strode to a chestnut mare and patted her shoulder.

Sir Lochlan stopped me from swinging myself up with the warning in his tone. "The prince thinks it safer for you to be in the carriage. The tunnels of Redrune are plagued with bandits and beggars. Sometimes they're desperate enough to threaten a large party, like ours."

I sighed as I stroked the horse's velvety nose. "What about Alyss and Grix?"

"Alyss will stay in the carriage with you and the prince. Grix is going to ride up front with me and half the guard."

I looked back at the carriage to see Grix already stepping out and walking toward us. Sir Lochlan led the mare away by the halter and passed the reins to Grix, who clambered up, obviously still sore from the last time he rode.

"Are you okay with this?" I asked as the chestnut horse danced a little, testing the experience of her rider.

"Of course," he said, jaw set. "I'll do whatever it takes to protect the prince and you girls."

Another guard led a blue roan to Sir Lochlan, who swung up easily in the saddle after grabbing the reins.

I watched for a moment as they guided their horses forward toward the tunnel. Only then did I realize that people were streaming out of it, dressed in rags. Desperate people.

And desperate people were dangerous people.

I hurried toward the carriage, where Alyss leaned out the door, her long black hair flowing in the wind as she stared after Grix. I watched her suspiciously. It seemed like the two had grown awfully close. When she heard me approach she ducked back inside, a rosy pink tint blooming on her cheeks.

I climbed up beside her and shut the door, finding myself face to face with Prince Matthias. "I was worried you wouldn't come down," he said. "Sir Lochlan whistled at least five times before you heard him."

"I'm sorry," I said as the carriage jumped forward. "I can fly lower next time."

The prince waved his hand idly. "It doesn't matter, as long as you make sure to keep an eye on us. Perhaps on cloudy days like this one, you should ride in the carriage."

I tensed, but nodded anyway. He hadn't taken away my privilege, only limited it.

Prince Matthias turned to Alyss. "What were we talking about before the carriage stopped?"

"The inn in Redrune," she answered.

I tuned out their conversation as I glanced out the window. It was only seconds before the scenic view of the misty mountains gave way to rocks, and then darkness as we entered the tunnel. The people streamed by the window, dozens of gaunt faces molding into a shadowy blur. I could hear the echo of the rattling carriage and the clopping horse hooves against the hard rock. My heart raced as the echoes gave way to shouting voices up ahead. The carriage slowed. Alyss clutched my hand with her small, cold one, worry creasing her forehead.

I glanced back out the window, straining to see what was ahead, but all I saw were the men, women, and children. Most of them were watching the commotion up ahead with dead, unfeeling expressions. But one little girl, her hair framing her face in greasy brown spirals, stared right at me with pleading blue eyes, a small wooden bowl clutched in hand.

I was pitched into a childhood memory, one where I was a little girl, holding an empty wooden bowl. Unlike the memory of holding my mother's hand in a meadow, this one was something I'd remembered since the day it happened. When the caretaker of the orphan girls had been Madam Lorraine, a ruthless woman with a permanent gash of a frown, straight, bone-white hair, and irises such a light blue, they nearly blended in with the milky whites of her eyes.

The orphanage was new to me. New and cold and frightening. The creak of the floorboards, the screaming winter wind outside the window, and the hunger that gnawed at my empty belly kept me awake at night. I always imagined that the shadows were more than shadows. That they were watching me, waiting for my eyes to close before they would grab me and drag me to the dark depths from where they came.

Every morning, after those sleepless nights, the other young girls and I were sent out on the streets to beg for money. Sometimes people felt sorry for us and took us into their homes to warm up, but most days, we stayed outside until we reached our quota of three coins. On one of those days, many of the girls had already received their quota and gone back to the orphanage. The only one left besides me was another young girl about my age. Helen.

We clutched each other for warmth, our bowls placed down in the snow, slowly sinking deeper as fresh flakes fell from the sky. At one point, they were buried so deep I had to bend over and dig them out. I had handed Helen her bowl, while I held mine in my icy fingers, the melting snow already seeping its way through my mittens. People sought refuge in homes and taverns, and I knew we would have to return to the orphanage without the rest of our money.

"We should go," I said to Helen through chattering teeth and blue lips.

"L-let this man pass, and th-then we'll leave," she said, her voice even shakier than mine.

I looked toward the end of the street in hope. If he was generous, he would spare us both a whipping. He approached us with hands in his pockets. He had graying hair, crinkled eyes, and a carefree look about him. For a moment, I thought that he was going to pass us by, but then he paused. And turned back.

"Why are you out here, in the weather? You should be inside, by a warm fire." His voice was smooth, silky.

"W-we can't go back to the o-orphanage until we reach q-quota," chattered Helen.

His face showed concern. "Why don't you both come with me? My wife and daughter are preparing venison stew. The house will be toasty warm." His voice rose and fell playfully.

A shiver tickled its way down my spine, but this time, it wasn't the cold.

Helen let herself smile, gratitude clouding her blue eyes. "W-we would very much enjoy that, wouldn't we, Ivy?" She looked at me, her brown tangles draped messily over her shoulder.

I gave a small shake of my head. "We should go back. If we aren't there by lunchtime, we'll get a whipping," I said.

The man waited for Helen to make a decision. To go with her friend or to take him up on his offer.

She shook her head at me and slipped her hand into the man's. "How old is your daughter?" she asked, looking up at him.

He passed me a fleeting glance, but started to walk away with Helen. "She's probably a few years older than you, dear."

I watched helplessly as they walked away. Part of me wanted to go with them, to make sure Helen stayed safe. But I just turned in the direction of the orphanage, wading back slowly through the snow. I was rewarded with a spanking and no lunch.

The rest of the day, Helen was gone. At dinner, she still hadn't returned. At bedtime, the bed beside mine was empty. The next day they found her, buried in a pile of bloodied snow, stiff as a block of ice. Madam Lorraine disappeared before the law called on her, no doubt fleeing for Kislow while all the little orphan girls dealt with their grief.

I never told anyone that I'd let the man take her. Never met anyone's questions with more than silence.

After that day, my nights were so much worse.

Because in the shadows, Helen lurked.

Chapter Eight

By THE TIME I came back up from my trance, the darkness of the tunnel had disappeared and we'd emerged into the misty day. Small huts surrounded us now, dotting the crater of Redrune. Sheep chewed on the grass, watching lazily as we passed them by.

Alyss was holding my hand, her voice tender as she asked, "Are you okay?"

I slipped my hand away, smiling even through my discomfort. "Yes, I was just...caught up in a memory. Do you know what slowed us in the tunnel?"

She nodded. "There was another carriage coming out of Redrune, but the tunnel wasn't wide enough for us to pass them. They had to back out."

"I was wondering what was going on in your head," the prince broke in. "Was it a good memory or a bad memory?"

"A bad one," I said. I watched the sheep as they grazed. Watched the men as they mended fences and the women chasing after children. Prince Matthias, with all his riches, could do something about those people in the tunnel. I turned my gaze on him. "Couldn't we help them?"

The prince shrugged uncomfortably. "Most of those people are poor by their own actions. They may have been alcoholics or gamblers."

"Not the children," I said. "The children are innocent."

"What can we do? If we give the children money, their parents will spend it...and we can't exactly take the children away from their families."

Alyss spoke up. "What about a soup kitchen? The crown could fund it."

The prince rubbed his stubbly chin. "My father is tight with his money, especially now...but it's not a bad idea. I may mention it to him when we get there."

The carriage started to rattle as the road we traveled on gave way to a more uneven path. We bounced along uncomfortably until the rocks all around us disappeared, replaced by cliff-face so close that if I opened the door, it would hit the stone. Several minutes passed and the cliff began to distance itself. Finally, buildings appeared again.

The carriage stopped in front of a large castle-like building with large pillars and a beautiful mahogany door.

I looked forward to going inside, but before I could follow the others, Sir Lochlan stepped in front of me. "We need to go see my family," he said, his face pale and grim.

My heart sunk as I thought back on Roland's death and the promise I'd made him. Now it was time to keep that promise.

I followed him to the chestnut mare and hoisted myself up, waiting patiently as Sir Lochlan adjusted the stirrups to match my height. When he was done, he swung onto his roan and we were off.

We continued through the rest of the city. It didn't take very long. While Redrune looked quite impressive from the outside, it wasn't as big as Achron. More huts began to dot the hills as the larger buildings faded away.

The farther we got, the more spread out they became until we sidled up to a small cabin with a sizable garden. Nearby, a few wooly faces peeped out of a shed in curiosity. A chilly mist began to fall from the sky, seeping the cold down to my bones. Even though the glow of a warm fire flickered invitingly in the window, I dreaded going inside to meet Roland's family.

"This is it?" I asked, stopping my horse beside Sir Lochlan's.

He nodded. "Seems a little small for a family of seven doesn't it?"

I didn't reply as I dismounted the mare. Sir Lochlan followed suit. He led the way up the stairs while I cowered behind. Before he could even knock, the door was flung open. Golden light outlined a silhouette of a thin woman. "Loch? Is that really you?"

"Yes, Mother." He stood in front of her awkwardly, his head lowered.

She choked out a cry and wrapped him in a hug. "Oh, Lochlan, you have no idea how much I've missed you."

She pulled back and seemed to see me for the first time. She squinted her eyes. "Is this the fiancée you wrote about? I thought you said she had black hair."

Sir Lochlan shook his head. "No. Celia is back at the castle."

It impressed me to hear about Celia. I didn't think Sir Lochlan had much of a soft side, but apparently, he did.

"This is Ivy," Sir Lochlan said. "She went to the Crescent Isle Conservatory."

"Oh?" his mom asked. "You must know Roland then." Worry lines etched into her forehead when I looked away quickly without a reply.

Sir Lochlan looked past her, into the house. "Is Father or any of the others home?"

"Your father is out at sea," she replied. "Brent is upstairs, he's here for the weekend, and Kayta is here with her son while her husband is building their house in Silvonville. Jake is at the castle, of course, and Roland..." she trailed off as her eyes flicked to me. She wrung her hands nervously.

Sir Lochlan swallowed tightly and let out a strangled breath. "Roland is why we're here, Mama."

"What's happened?" she asked, her voice barely above a whisper.

Sir Lochlan placed a hand on her shoulder and led her back into the house. I followed hesitantly. At the sight of Lochlan, a woman—who I assumed was Kayta—stood up, holding a sleeping newborn in her arms.

Her mouth formed into a small smile until she registered the grim facial expressions on both her mother and brother. "What's wrong?" she asked. She looked at me, her eyes narrowed in distrust.

I heard more footsteps sound above us. They became louder as they descended the stairs. A man that looked exactly like an older version of Roland appeared at the bottom. He studied each face very carefully until he came to mine.

"What is it?" he asked, his fierce eyes boring into my own.

I opened my mouth, but closed it again before I said something I'd regret. Why had he asked me? Why not his brother? I looked at Sir Lochlan for help.

"I asked the girl," Brent snapped before Sir Lochlan could say anything.

Sir Lochlan pressed his mouth into a firm line, his eyes narrowing at his brother before he turned back to me. Every eye in the room was on me, save the newborn's.

I took in a deep, steadying breath. "Roland and I were sent on a quest to the Isle of Ginsey. When we got there, the natives shot us with darts dipped in a sleeping draft." I cleared my throat, not wanting to get choked up with emotion. "Roland had an allergic reaction...he didn't make it."

My words were met by shocked silence. There was one more thing I needed to say. "He wanted me to tell you that he went to live in a place without fear or worry or anguish. He even got a glimpse of it before he died." Tears pricked my eyes.

Lochlan's mother's face was as white as a sheet as she held his arm in a death grip. He led her to a chair and set her down gently.

Kayta's baby began to wail, but Kayta just stared straight ahead, her eyes glassed over with unshed tears.

Brent eyes were narrowed accusingly, and he took a threatening step toward me. Sir Lochlan pried his mother's fingers off his arm to step in front of his brother. "Brent, it's not her fault."

Brent looked at Lochlan, his lip curled in anger. Before I had time to think about my actions, I bolted out the door, slamming it behind me. I changed in midstride, lifting off into the air. I couldn't help the untamed cries of sadness that escaped me as I flew higher.

Sir Lochlan's words echoed through my mind. "Brent, it's not her fault," he'd said.

But I can't stop thinking that it is. If only I'd just gone alone.

It is my fault.

Chapter Nine

Sir Lochlan called after me as I flew over the rocky hills, but I paid him no mind. The hotel wasn't hard to find. It was easily the largest building in Redrune.

I folded in my wings and angled downward, plunging into a seemingly vacant alleyway. I landed on human feet and leaned against the stone wall to steady myself.

What have I done? Of all the times I'd thought of telling Roland's family about his death, nothing could have been worse than what really happened. I'd kept my promise to Roland, but I ran away like a feeble mouse at the first sign of danger.

I took in a deep breath and pushed myself away from the wall, walking swiftly around the corner to get back to the mahogany doors. I gripped the handle, but instantly jerked it away when it started to smoke. A glowing orange hand print was seared into the metal. I took in a deep breath to calm myself and opened the door quickly, elbowing it shut once I was inside.

The foyer was grand, with the ceiling stretched high above my head. Blue and silver banners with the king's insignia lined the hall. Flickering lanterns were hung on either side of each one, to the very end of the wide corridor. I took a few steps forward, and as I walked, the lanterns on either side of me went out one by one. I paused as the rest of the lights went out until I was all alone in a darkened corridor. Only the moonlight lit the way to the empty desk and the doors just beyond it.

My heartbeat skipped. I was still in first form, and yet somehow, power trickled through to my human body. I was absorbing the heat. I walked toward one of the unlit lanterns and cupped my hands around it, willing it to relight. A bolt of fire struck the lantern, glass and metal shrapnel shooting everywhere. All that was left was a blackened spot on the wall.

I jumped when someone cleared their throat at the other end of the hallway. Grix stood in the doorway, his hand still on the doorknob.

"I'm guessing things didn't go well?" he asked, studying the charred remains of the lantern.

I hid my stinging hands behind me. "No, they didn't," I said in a small voice.

He shut the door and came closer. "What happened?"

I didn't want to talk about it. I turned away.

"Come on, was it that bad?" he said.

"I ran away," I said, fighting back tears.

"Why?"

"Well, Roland's brother threatened me, but that's only part of it." I paused. "I ran away because I couldn't stand to see the pain on their faces for one moment longer before I…" I trailed off.

"Before you broke down, too?" Grix finished for me.

I looked back at him, trying to keep the tears from falling. "It was hard for me to lose him, but them? They had twenty years of knowing him, of watching him grow from a child into a man. And I keep feeling like I could have done something to spare them that pain."

He put his hand on my shoulder in an awkward gesture to comfort me. "There was nothing you could do, or you would've done it. The past it over, so let's live for the present and the future. What would Roland want you to do right now?"

"I'm not sure."

Grix rubbed the back of his neck. "My bet is that he'd want you to take a deep breath and calm yourself…and then, he'd want you to go eat something before you starve to death."

I laughed, and the tension in the room immediately lifted. All at once the lanterns relit, filling the hall with light.

He glanced at the lanterns and gave me a tight smile. "You're getting stronger, Ivy. You need to control your emotions if this is what they can do. Perhaps a way you can cope with it for now is that question—*what would Roland want you to do?*"

He led the way back to the door he'd come through. "The dining hall has been cleared and everyone's gone up to their rooms. I'm sure we can find something in the kitchen, though."

He opened the door and let me slip past him.

Alyss was standing right inside, a worried expression on her face. "What was that sound?"

"It was just me," I said. Unsure of how she would take the fact that I'd blown something up, I stopped there.

"She made a lantern explode," Grix interrupted.

I shot him a look that he shrugged off.

Alyss's eyes widened as she looked back at me. "How?"

"It was an accident," I said. "I was trying to relight it."

"And because she was angry, it disintegrated instead," Grix added.

I glared at him and he raised his hands defensively.

"I didn't disintegrate it," I muttered.

Alyss gave me a worried smile.

"Let's just go find something to eat," I said, and walked past her into a room full of tables. A dining hall. Just beyond that was a door that I guessed led to the kitchens. When I opened it, the smells wafting up the stairs confirmed my assumption. Freshly baked cookies.

When the cook heard that I hadn't eaten anything, he gathered together a tray of sliced meat, breads, and fruits. Not surprisingly, Grix ate most of it, though he claimed to have already eaten.

After I'd finished, Alyss led me up to where I was supposed to sleep, in a room adjacent to hers. It was nicely furnished, with a four-poster bed, a trunk, two chairs on either side of a window, and a table lined with books right between them. As soon as Alyss left for her own room, I sighed and tiredly headed over to one of the chairs. I flopped down and rested my elbow on the arm as I studied the titles of the books.

Most of them were history books about Leviatha, but one in particular stood out to me. *Stories of Leviatha Castle*. I reached forward, took it, and started flipping through the pages. There were many sketches of a white castle, built right over the water, and other pictures of different statues of sea serpents, like Roland. I flipped a little farther through the book. There were brilliant gardens, an aquarium, and a myriad of ships docked right next to the castle. *King Horace IV's personal fleet,* the last picture was titled.

I turned the page to see a sketch of a princess on a balcony, her eyes wild with fear, smoke billowing out from the doorway behind her. The picture was titled, *The story of King Horace IV's daughter, Princess Rayna, and her new husband, Lord Vincent the Vicious.* Next to it, there was a poem.

It flickers and flutters and sputters and twists,
It pops and crackles and sizzles and roars.
The mighty dance of the beast called Fire
climbs higher and higher up the castle spire,
where a princess with a long white veil
tightly grips the balcony rail.
Where is her prince?
Will he come to save her?
The truth is he won't,
for he's the pied piper,
coaxing the flame, the cold-blooded viper.
He'll steal her inheritance,
he'll steal her throne,
but what he doesn't know is that the princess isn't alone.
Fire is ruthless,
and Fire is his fate.
He tries to get out,
but it's just too late.
Their spirits leave their bodies,
their earthly lives have ceased,

but one flies skyward,

above the flame and to the feast.

The other is dragged below where he dances,

an agonizing dance with the Fire Beast.

I shuddered and closed the book. The bed was starting to look really comfy. Just looking at it made my eyes droop shut. I stood, lumbered across the room, and crawled under the covers, letting myself drift slowly away.

My subconscious took me back to Lochlan's house. In the dream, instead of Brent being the only one glaring at me threateningly, all of Roland's family gave me accusing looks. Even Sir Lochlan. I backed away, just like I had in real life, but this time, my foot bumped into something. I looked down to see Roland's pale, cold face staring up at me lifelessly.

I wanted to scream, but couldn't, and when I looked back up at Roland's family, they were all closing in on me. There was no one there to stop Brent this time as he wrapped his calloused hands around my neck and…

Bang, bang, bang! I jerked awake as soon as I heard the deafening sound of a heavy fist slamming into the door. My heart beat furiously in my chest. I rushed to open the door only to be met with the sight of Sir Lochlan's livid expression, highlighted by the lantern he held in his white-knuckled fist.

Chapter Ten

I NARROWED MY eyes and turned away as I went back to sit on my bed.

"What do you want?" I asked, bracing myself for whatever Sir Lochlan had come to say.

He barged inside, leaving the door open. "How dare you run like that!" he snarled. "I couldn't even stay to comfort my family because I was too worried that you hadn't returned. Do you know what the king would have done to me if I failed to bring you back? The future you would leave my fiancée and me?"

I paled. "You didn't have to worry—"

"How would I know that?" he broke in. "All you've wanted to do since we took you from the conservatory is get away from everyone. You went on a walk and got attacked by bandits. You decided to fly up ahead this morning, which made me have to keep an eye on you the entire time to make sure you stayed with us. And now, you run away at the slightest hint of aggressiveness from my brother? He wouldn't have even hurt you, nor would he be able to. If you're not immortal, you're nearly there!"

I balled my fists at my sides. "You of all people should understand why I want to be alone. You intimidate everyone, and push them away with your miserable attitude."

"It's my job to intimidate people!" he shouted.

As soon as I picked up the scent of smoke, I stood and looked back at the bed. Sure enough, there were two holes burned through the quilt where my hands had been. I shook with rage as I turned back to Sir Lochlan. "Get out of my room," I said, eyes flashing.

He took one look at what I'd done to my blanket and stepped back, the ire slipping from his features. "We'll talk about this tomorrow," he said warily, and then strolled out the door, shutting it loudly behind him.

I sighed heavily, and crawled back in bed. It took a while for my anger to calm down, but after what seemed like an hour, I started to drift off again.

And then I heard three more pounds on the door. I threw the covers off and stomped across the room, ready for another round of arguments with Lochlan. I flung the door open only to find Grix there. And his face was ashen.

My anger melted away like the snow. "What's wrong?"

"There's a fire. T-the entire inn is on fire."

Only then did the rippling roar of an insatiable blaze register in my hearing. I nearly tripped over Grix when I rushed out the door, into the smoking hallway. "Where is Alyss?" I asked.

"I made sure she was safely outside," he said.

"And the prince?"

We stumbled backward as one of the support beams suddenly crashed down, exposing the fiery inferno of the third floor. Grix swallowed hard. "Upstairs," he said, pointing.

"Make sure everyone on this hallway and downstairs gets out safely. I'll go upstairs for the prince."

He nodded, and before I could see where he went, I sprinted to the end of the hall and bounded up the steps. Already, I could feel the heat getting more intense. I burst through the door at the top. My eyes and mind focused as the flames circled around me. All of a sudden, through all that heat and fire, I could see a figure crouching at the end of the hallway, their arm covering their face as they tried to get to my end of the hallway. I walked forward, clearing the way through the flame. Sir Lochlan squinted up at me. Several burn marks were seared into his hands, and the tips of his hair were singed.

"Ivy..." he coughed out. "The prince...he's in the room at the end of the hall. We have to save him."

I looked at the large flaming door. There was no way that Lochlan could save him now. Only I could. I looked back at Lochlan. Even after everything that he'd put me through, I couldn't just leave him in the hallway to die.

I grabbed his shirt and hauled him over my shoulder.

He shouted in surprise. "What? Put me down!"

I cleared the path to the door, and pushed the flame away from it, so that it wouldn't hurt Sir Lochlan when we ducked through the frame.

I turned the scorching-hot handle and swung the door wide. The entire room was ablaze. My eyes searched the room for Prince Matthias, but all they found were his empty bed. The blankets, dragged to the other side as if someone had fallen off. I hurried over and set Lochlan down on the ground. He glared at me through tired eyes. I could tell he was doing all he could to stay awake after inhaling so much smoke.

I hurried to the other side of the bed, tossing aside the covers to see Matthias hidden partly under the bed, a bloody gash in the side of his head.

"Oh, no," I said as I tossed the blanket away. Just outside the door, I heard another crash and the entire building jolted as if it were on the verge of collapse.

I didn't have time to check the prince's pulse to see if he was alive. All I could do was lift his unconscious body and place him next to where Sir Lochlan lay, now barely conscious.

I knew we had to escape fast, or else go down with the fiery building. Hurriedly, I grabbed a blazing chair and swung it at a stained glass window. The glass shattered on impact, and the firelight twinkled over the surface of the shards as they fell to the ground. It was simple to shift form when I was surrounded by flame already. I gripped Prince Matthias with my claws, and pulled his limp body down to the window. With a great heft of my wings, I dove through the opening, trying not to catch Matthias's body on the glass shards that still stuck up in the frame. From down below, a collected gasp sounded. It seemed like nearly half the city was up, watching as the greatest building in their midst burned down in flames.

I sunk down and dropped the prince to the ground at the edge of the crowd, and a few people rushed forward to help him.

I circled back into the window and spiraled through it, landing heavily next to Sir Lochlan, who had lost his battle to stay conscious.

I gripped his shoulders tightly, but before I could lift him up, the ceiling above us collapsed. I stretched my wings out over Sir Lochlan just before a flaming support beam crashed down on top of me. Had I not had unnatural strength, Lochlan and I would've both been crushed.

The flames burned hot along my back. If I didn't find a way to get Sir Lochlan out soon, he would die. I gathered all my strength and threw the beam off of me. It shifted and rolled to the side, the flames finding the blanket that the prince had been wrapped in just moments before. I grabbed a hold of Lochlan's shoulders once again, and pulled him out of the building with me.

The crowd stared in awe as I came back down, carrying yet another body. I laid Sir Lochlan next to where I had laid the prince.

When I looked over at Prince Matthias, my heart sunk with dread. A gray blanket was covering his body, the sure sign that there was no hope for him. That his heart had stopped.

I shifted form, tears already staining my face. "He's dead?" I asked the woman that stood over him protectively, her face grim.

"I'm afraid so," she said as she moved over to help Sir Lochlan.

I stifled a sob. "What will the king do to Sir Lochlan when he learns of his death?"

The woman gave me a strange look. "He'll probably just replace the man he lost."

"What?" I asked.

"I'm sure this soldier was a good man, but the king will just put a new one in his place. When they go to serve the king, they knowingly sacrifice their lives for him."

The meaning behind her words began to dawn on me.

I reached for the blanket and peeled it back to expose the charred and bloodied face of one of the guards that had helped escort us on our journey.

I still felt sadness and horror, but there was also guilty relief. The building behind me creaked and groaned as more of the roof caved in to the flames.

"Where was--" I paused and gritted my teeth as a few of my bones snapped painfully back in place. Slightly out of breath from the pain, I repeated, "Where was the prince taken?"

"He was carried off a few moments ago to the healer's house a few blocks from here," she said.

"This is his personal guard," I said, gesturing to Sir Lochlan. "He should probably go to the same place."

She beckoned to a strong-looking man in the crowd who came forward willingly. "Take this man to Madam La Clair."

I nodded a thank you to the woman and then followed the man through the crowd and past several houses. When we reached a stone building with a small sign that swung in the wind, the man turned abruptly into an alleyway, and entered through a green door.

Only seven beds in the clinic were taken so far. The prince was in one, Grix in another, and the last five were taken up by men and women that I'd never seen, all of them victims of the fire.

A woman wearing an apron was bent over the prince's face, a damp cloth pressed to a nasty burn that scarred his cheek.

I let the burly man carry Lochlan to a bed while I checked on Prince Matthias. His eyes were closed, but his breathing was steady, if a little raspy sounding. I sighed in relief. The woman looked up through her long gray hair. "Is there something I can help you with?"

"When will he be awake?" I asked.

She paused what she was doing briefly to study me. "And who is asking?"

The man called over from Sir Lochlan's bedside. "That's the girl who saved him."

The woman nodded her head. "So you're the fire bird," she said as she went back to tending the prince.

"When will he be awake?" I repeated.

She dropped the dirty cloth in a bowl of reddish brown water and wrung it out again. "The damage of the smoke to his lungs was minor. He'll probably have a raspy voice for a few days, but the only real injuries are the burns on his face and hand. And the bump on his forehead where it was smashed in." She paused. "Tell me, how did that happen?"

"I don't know. He was like this when I found him lying on his back beside his bed."

"Hmm. Sounds like the fire might not have been an accident," she suggested, raising an eyebrow as she went back to bathing the prince's wound. "He should be up in an hour, and we can ask him if he remembers anything. I gave him some medicine to keep him under so that we can get him clean and comfortable without feeling much pain."

I looked away when a few coughs and a groan sounded in Sir Lochlan's direction. His face was screwed up in pain.

I left the woman tending to Matthias and approached Lochlan's bed.

Another woman had come over to take care of him, pushing him back down into a laying position softly, while setting a cloth and a bowl of steaming water on the table beside them. Sir Lochlan pushed her away, and swung his feet over the side of the bed. "I'll be fine," he growled. On unsteady feet, he limped over to the prince.

I put a hand on his arm, but he jerked it away. "Don't touch me," he rasped. "You're probably the one who set the fire anyway."

I dropped my hand to my side, hurt that he would think that. "I did *not* start that fire," I said, trying to keep my voice from rising.

"How can you be sure of that? You don't even know how to control your power."

I blanched, knowing he was right. After all that had happened last night, I was an emotional mess.

What if I was the cause of the fire?

Chapter Eleven

I STEPPED OUT of the hospital into a smoky, lantern-lit street, crowded with people like it was market day instead of after midnight. Some were headed back from the fire, returning to their homes, while others were headed toward it, eyes wide at the wreckage down the street. I followed the newcomers, back to the inn which had collapsed in a giant heap of burning rubble.

Some people were crying, some stood stock-still, and some glared at the remaining debris. Drawn to the fire, I brushed past the onlookers and almost didn't recognize Alyss with her hair pulled back and her face darkened with ashy soot.

She'd noticed me before I noticed her. "Ivy!" she called. She dodged around people to get to me. "Have you seen Grix?"

"He was in the infirmary," I said, pointing back to the sign above the building.

Her eyes widened. "Is he okay?"

I bit my lip. *Why didn't I go check on him before I left?* "I think so...You'd better go see for yourself." I gestured to a burn on her arm with a grimace. "Get that seen to while you're at it."

She nodded and took off. I watched her until she opened the door and slipped inside. That's when I felt a tap on my shoulder. "Excuse me!"

I turned, surprised to find a man who stood eye to eye with me, his mouth turned downward like a toad's. Usually, men towered over me. "Yes?"

He scrutinized me. "You are the fire bird? The one who saved the prince?"

I nodded. "I am."

His toad frown became a smile. "I'd like to offer you and the prince and...whoever accompanies him...a place to stay."

I tried, and probably failed, to return his smile. "The prince and his personal guard might stay in the infirmary until we leave, but I'm sure the rest would be very grateful to you."

His smile faltered slightly. "A shame, since I would gladly show a member of the royal family my hospitality. But the offer still stands."

"Where is it?" I asked.

He looked down the street, thick eyebrows raised. "Not far from here. Just around the corner."

"Would you show me?" I said, glad to have something to do.

He puffed out his chest and led me away from the fire. "This way."

I followed him closely, and when we turned the corner, the street ahead was much clearer, but not as well-lit as the last. We came upon a row of tall, connected houses, gray and looming in the moonlight. The last on the row was the only one with a sign plastered to the front and glowing windows like cat eyes.

The man walked up the steps and opened the door, inviting me in. The fireplace lit up a large common room with three plush sofas, some armchairs, and a long dining table. A woman and two young girls sat on one the sofas in their nightclothes, but all three had shoes on. They'd obviously come from the fire.

The woman looked up when we entered. "You found her. And what about the prince?"

The man gestured for me to continue in the hallway while he talked to—I assumed—his wife.

The little girls watched me with big eyes until there was a wall separating us. There were four doors in the hallway, each of them open to empty bedrooms. Two of them were crowded with bunk beds, while both of the others held a larger bed, plenty of room for Alyss, Grix—if he was well enough—the remaining guards, and me. The quilts were old and the furniture worn, but it would do.

A rickety staircase led up to the second floor, but before I could get up the first step, the man called from the other end of the hallway. "Upstairs is where we sleep, but all the downstairs rooms are open to you."

I looked back at him. "This is very kind of you. We'll gladly accept your hospitality."

He smiled and let me brush past him on my way to the front door.

"My family and I are headed up to bed, so make yourselves at home when you get back," he called before I shut the door behind me.

When I returned to the scene of the fire, it didn't take long for me to round up all the guards, especially since after I'd found the first one, he helped track down all the others. Most had been mourning over their fallen comrade, and when they heard of the place to stay, they followed behind me with the dead body in tow. *The innkeeper probably won't like that.*

I was about to check in the infirmary for Alyss and Grix when they walked out. I waved them over, and they joined our ranks, faces grave when they saw the body. A couple guards departed from our group and headed into the hospital, no doubt to check on Prince Matthias and Sir Lochlan.

Grix's entire arm, which he held against his chest, was bandaged up and the ends of his hair had been singed in the fire.

He noticed me studying him and lifted his eyebrows. "Where are we going?"

I looked down at my feet as we followed the cobblestone road. "Another inn. We'll probably be staying there more than one night so that everyone can recover."

He waited a while before he asked, "What happened after we separated?"

I explained finding Sir Lochlan and the prince, adding that I'd found the prince already wounded and tucked halfway under the bed.

A dark look cast over his features. "Sounds suspicious to me. Makes me think the fire was started to kill the prince…or at least to give us a scare."

That was the only thing that kept me from blaming myself. "And what about you?" I asked.

"I checked all the rooms I could before I had to get out. I only saved two more people."

"Thank you, Grix," I said. "If you hadn't awoken me, the prince and Lochlan would probably be dead right now."

He shrugged. "It's a miracle I was conscious enough to hear the fire."

Later that night—which I'm sure was actually early morning—I took out the phantom stone and studied it. Large, dirty fingerprints were still visible on the glossy surface. I wiped them away with the hem of my dress and decided it was as good a time as any to check on Kurt.

The cool chain grazed over my face as I slipped it on and was sucked from my body, back into the weightless spirit world. I appeared next to Kurt, who was lying face down in a pile of moldy hay. Through the bloody rips in his shirt, his back was covered in deep gashes. The sight sent shivers running through my translucent form.

My gaze flitted around the room. Instead of the dark dungeon, silvery moonlight lit up a hexagon-shaped cell. I assumed he was back in the north tower.

I stared at the motionless figure that was my brother. "Kurt?"

One tired, green eye flickered open.

I drifted closer. "Are you okay?"

He studied me for a moment before pushing himself up onto his elbows gingerly, wincing at the pain. "I've had worse."

I bit my lip. "Did you tell them anything about me?"

His eyes darted away. "I told them that your favorite weapon was the sword."

True. I'd never had the same bond with any other weapon. But they'd probably already known that. "That's it?"

"No…" he sighed, his expression haggard as he studied his bloodied and mutilated fingernails. "Once I let one thing out, they increased the pain levels. If I could take it back, I would, but I said the worst thing possible. I let them get the best of me."

"What did you say?" I asked, fear rooting itself in my mind.

His temple pulsed as he gritted his teeth. "I was desperate. I-I told them that you had immortality running through your veins. That each day you grow more and more powerful, and it won't be long before you destroy them… They deserve it, Ivy. Do you even know what those guards have done to women and children in the dungeons?"

Chills wavered through my spirit. "But how can that information be used against me?"

"They know that I've been communicating with someone outside the castle. It's only a matter of time before they figure out how."

It took me a second to realize what he was implying. "Are you saying that we should stop communicating?"

He closed his eyes. "Yes. If they find out about the phantom stone, that puts you in danger. They'll use it to spy on you."

"But this is the only way I can keep track of how you're doing," I whispered. "How will I know if you're alive in the future?"

"It's better for me to die than the both of us," he replied. I shook my head in protest, but he continued on. "As soon as you take it off and return to where you came from, you need to bury it or throw it in a river. Keep it far from you."

My heart ached, but I managed to say, "What will happen with your pendant if they find it?"

"Hopefully, it will lead them to the middle of the forest or at the bottom of a lake. It depends on where you leave yours." He looked at the door suspiciously. "You should go. The sorcerers may be able to sense your presence."

I nodded. "You may be right," I said quietly. I studied his gaunt face one last time. "Just in case something bad happens... I love you, Kurt."

His shaded eyes sparkled with tears as he said, "I love you, too. And Ivy?"

"Yes?"

"Whatever the prophecy says, whatever you're supposed to do...I believe in you."

I didn't even believe in myself, but I accepted his words with a nod. Then, I took off the necklace, and the weight of the world pressed on my shoulders once again.

I pushed myself up off the mattress and tip-toed out of my bedroom into the hall, Kurt's words still ringing in my head. I peeked into the common room, and when I saw there was no one, I made my way to the front door. I tried my hardest to open it softly, cringing when the hinges creaked loudly.

A few heartbeats later, I slipped outside, shutting the door as quietly as possible. Out in the open, I breathed a sigh of relief, and started my trek toward the edge of town, the pendant swinging in my hand as I walked. As soon as I'd made it onto one of the little farms, I ducked through a fence and made my way through the long, swaying grass to the middle of the field. I stooped down and began digging with my hands, unearthing the rocky soil. My nails cracked and chipped, but they were already healing by the time I'd dug deep enough. I dropped the phantom stone into the shallow pit. It glinted up at me in the moonlight.

As I began to replace the dirt, I suddenly felt as if I was being watched. I looked up, scanning my surroundings, but I was completely alone. I packed the dirt down tightly and stood, retracing my steps back to the inn, where I creaked open the door and slid back into my room, seemingly undetected.

Chapter Twelve

THE NEXT DAY, I awoke to a knock on the door. I pushed my tangles back and opened it to find Prince Matthias standing there in full uniform with a bandage wrapped around his head. I blushed, imagining what a sight I was this morning.

He didn't seem to care, his eyes warm as he said, "May I come in?" His voice was raspy, but not nearly as bad as I expected.

I stood aside. "Of course."

Behind him, I saw the innkeeper, looking thrilled to have the prince in his home before the door was shut in his face.

"I didn't mean to wake you," the prince said. "I suppose I should have guessed you'd be asleep after everything that happened last night—everything I can't remember."

He seemed too close in the small room, so I retreated to the bed and started pulling up the covers. "It's not a problem. But what time is it?"

"Nearly two in the afternoon," he said as he watched me. "Anyway, I just wanted to thank you for saving me from the fire."

I stiffened and looked up at him, hoping he wouldn't blame me for what happened last night like Sir Lochlan had. "I just did what anyone else would do," I said with a shrug. I smoothed the covers and turned to face him as he walked over and leaned against the bedpost.

His face was serious as he looked me in the eye. "I'm in your debt, Ivy. I hope to be able to repay you someday."

I avoided his gaze. "There's no need for that."

I flinched when he took a step forward and rested both hands on my shoulders. "I *will* repay you," he said, his face so close that I could see every freckle that dotted his nose.

His gaze flicked down to study my lips. When I started to take a step back, he dropped his hands and strolled to the door. "We'll be taking the day off to bury Lukas. I'll let you know when the hole is dug."

"Um…thank you," I said awkwardly as the door clicked shut. Below the door, I saw his shadow pause briefly, and then his footsteps continued on down the hallway, leaving me with my confused thoughts. I was tempted to lay back down in the bed, but hunger got the best of me.

Only Alyss and a few guards were in the common room when I came out. Alyss sat at the table, bent over a piece of paper as she scribbled on it with charcoal.

I sat down across from her, catching a glimpse of a sketched bird in an iron cage. "What are you working on?" I asked.

She looked up in surprise and covered her drawing with her hand. "Oh, nothing. I figured I would sketch while I had the time."

"Can I see?"

She bit her lip, but nodded and pushed the piece of paper over to me.

There was a cage, but now that I looked closely, I could see that it was old and rusted, with holes in several spots. The little door to the cage was open, and yet the little bird she'd drawn was still sitting there, content. "It's beautiful."

She whisked the drawing back and stared at it. She opened her mouth to say something else, but the innkeeper's wife was already speaking from behind me.

"Would you like something to eat?"

I looked back at her, seeing that, if possible, she appeared more frazzled than she had last night. Her apron was covered in flour and her formerly pinned back hair was falling out of place.

"Yes, thank you," I replied.

She hurried into the kitchen and came back out a minute later with plate of chicken, green beans, and a piece of bread.

Alyss went back to her sketches while I dug into the meal. The woman cleared my plate when I was done, and for the first time in a long time, I was able to relax as I watched Alyss add more details to her sketch. The guards that gathered around the fireplace talked, sometimes laughing, and for a moment, everything felt light and happy.

And then the door creaked open, and the prince stepped inside to say the two words that darkened everyone's mood. "It's time."

The next five days after Lukas's funeral passed by slowly. Every breath we breathed was either road dust—until we could feel the grit between our teeth—or saltwater spray. I usually got to fly whenever I felt like it and when it rained, Grix, Alyss, the prince, and I stayed in the carriage while Sir Lochlan volunteered to ride out in the downpour with the rest of the guard, claiming it didn't bother him.

He and the guard were constantly on high alert ever since the fire, and unlike the prince, Sir Lochlan never thanked me for saving his life.

On the last day, when we finally boarded the final ship, I was relieved, but at the same time, apprehensive about meeting the king and staying in the castle. At least when we traveled, I got to fly every once in a while. Would I be trapped in a stone structure for days until I left for my quest?

As we neared land, I could see the giant castle that dwarfed the buildings and hills around it.

I stood with my elbows on the rail of the ship when Prince Matthias approached me and rested one of his hands in the rail next to me while the other pointed into the distance.

"Do you see that tower? The tallest one in the front?"

I squinted my eyes and nodded.

He dropped his hand to the rail. "My father once kept me in that tower for two weeks after I disguised myself as a villager and took a stroll through the streets. I never saw why he got so angry."

I shrugged. "It might be dangerous for someone like you to be out there."

He turned his back to the castle and looked down at me. "It didn't stop me from doing it again. I just made sure not to get caught."

I shook my head and smiled. "Of course you did...but why did you want to disguise yourself anyway?"

He shrugged. "I like the perks of being a prince. The food, the servants, the parties, and of course, access to the stables and the royal marina. But every once in a while, I just liked to get away from the duties and the fake smiles and the bowing and curtsying."

"Sounds like something I would do," I said, thinking of what Sir Lochlan had said days before, how I was always trying to get away.

He stared at me intently as his hand inched closer to mine on the railing. "We're more alike than you think."

I cringed inwardly, but pretended not to notice as I turned to Alyss and Grix. "I'd better go see if those two are ready to dock."

I felt cowardly for retreating, but any feelings I had quickly evaporated when I realized that Alyss and Grix were holding hands, standing so close to one another that if they stepped one inch further, someone's toes would get stepped on. As I watched, Grix leaned forward slowly, hesitantly, and kissed Alyss right on the mouth.

It would have been sweet…had I not been trying to get away from Prince Matthias for the very same reason. I fled like a rabbit, hating that I could only go as far as the other side of the ship.

In my effort to keep my eyes averted from the embracing couple, I glanced back at the prince. His mouth formed a half smile as he watched me.

Frustration clawed at my insides and I tightened my jaw. I stared at him with cold, dead eyes, hoping to convey a specific message. *I'm not interested.*

He never looked away. In the end, I broke eye contact.

Chapter Thirteen

I'D THOUGHT I would want to be one of the first ones off the ship, but looking down into the crowd below, I reconsidered. A few guards went down the plank first, and the crowd may as well have been sharks waiting to greet them. When Prince Matthias followed after them, one girl managed to grab the sleeve of his uniform, pulling him into the crowd, but Sir Lochlan, always the prince's shadow, quickly forced her back. The prince, meanwhile, straightened his uniform and continued as if nothing had happened.

In the chaos, it was hard to tell if people were excited or angry, but with such a large assembly, I imagined it must be both. What a difference this was from the northern islands. We appreciated stories of the royal family up there, but we hardly reacted to anything with this much energy. Maybe the cold weather mellowed us out.

"You may want to get off now, while their attention is riveted to the prince," said one of the guards behind me.

It was true. There wasn't one person looking this way. I hurried down the plank, but could already feel the attention shift on me after Prince Matthias hoisted himself up into the carriage. I kept my eyes on the path ahead until I saw the prince's hand. The prince and his advances were nothing compared to a thunderous horde of people, so I took it and settled into the seat beside him.

Alyss and Grix were next. He led her down, eyes narrowed protectively while she kept her head bent, every now and then glancing up at the people with wide, owl eyes. Grix helped her inside, and then slammed the door shut as he joined the other guards, who would accompany us on horseback.

"Why are there so many?" Alyss asked as the carriage jolted forward.

"And why are they all screaming?" I added.

Prince Matthias shrugged. "It's always been like that here, though I can say the attendance of girls peaked when my brother and I turned sixteen."

"So they aren't mad?" Alyss asked, voicing one of my own questions.

"Of course not. Why should they be?" the prince asked.

I was tempted to spew out a few protests against the castes, but I bit my tongue. *This might not be the best time.*

The palace neared quickly, and at close range, it was beautiful. The color of the stone was the same color as the sand on the beach that stretched beyond it. Neatly trimmed green grass and evergreen bushes stood out against its grandeur. Graveled walkways crisscrossed over the grounds and several elegant fountains were lined up in front of the castle. Under each of the tall stained glass windows, a blue and silver flag whipped in the wind.

More guards and servants waited for us by the tall, open doors, most of them smiling and yet, others with faces of stone. And standing in front of them, ready to greet us on the bottom step, was the most stony-faced of them all. King Giddon.

As soon as the carriage lurched to a stop, a footman opened the door. "Wait here," the prince instructed quietly before he stepped out.

He walked up to his father and bowed low. The king let him stay that way for a while before he allowed him to stand back up with a few quiet words. I couldn't hear anything they were saying, but I could see their mouths moving, and after a while, the corners of the king's mouth lifted slightly.

I nearly jumped when King Giddon gestured in my direction, his eyes squinting as he took me in. Then, his smile grew bigger as he said something inaudible to Prince Matthias that made the prince look at his feet, the tips of his ears reddening. When the king started walking toward me, my heartbeat quickened. I'd heard tales of his bravery and his strength, but I'd never heard anything about his hospitality.

"You must be Ivy," he said, stopping a few feet away, hand gripping his sword hilt.

"Yes, sir." My eyes flickered to his hand as I tried to determine whether or not it was a threat.

He let his hand drop away from the sword and instead raised it toward the castle. "Come, let us walk inside together. There are many things we must discuss."

As soon as I stepped down from the carriage, he pressed the palm of his hand into my back, pushing me forward and up the stairs at a clipped pace. The prince followed closely until we were inside, but Alyss, Grix, and Sir Lochlan fell behind.

The king led the way through the crowded corridor, which was so full of people that the black and white checkered tile was barely visible. Servants and guards stared at me as I trailed behind him.

When we turned a corner, the crowd finally started to thin. With one peek back, I saw that the prince was still following, his face revealing nothing about what was to come.

We're very alike, you know, he'd said. In truth, no one could be more different from me than the prince. He was raised in a castle, has had servants going to and fro at his every beck and call since the day he was born. I was raised in an orphanage where I had to beg on the streets just to be able to eat.

As soon as we reached a single door with gold lining the edges, the king turned the knob and pushed it open to reveal an office with two plush chairs facing a desk peppered with papers, and behind the desk, a large tapestry of Erabyn. As soon as I—and a few moments later, the prince—stepped into the room, the king shut the door and turned the lock.

I bit my lip and circled around to the chair by the window, which overlooked the never-ending sea. Watching the waves lap at the shore calmed me considerably.

As Prince Matthias took a seat in the chair next to me, King Giddon strolled over and stood behind his desk. "You know why you're here, don't you?" he asked, placing his knuckles on the desktop as he watched me.

I shifted nervously. "Um…because the phoenix is part of some prophecy?"

"*You* are part of a prophecy. This isn't about the phoenix, girl. This is about you."

I flinched at the intensity of his words and nodded mutely.

"What do you know of the prophecy?" he continued.

I tilted my head. "I'm supposed to save the kingdoms?"

He crossed his arms. "It seems so. At least, that's what we've been told."

"What you've been told?" I questioned. "You don't know the entire prophecy?"

His broad shoulders lifted and sunk as he breathed in a deep sigh. "Unfortunately, no. We only have hints. Only the royal family of Onwin know the true prophecy."

"Then why am I not on my way there?" I asked, finding it difficult to hold in my annoyance.

"You'll get there in due time. Plus, I've invited one of them to stay at the palace. Princess Cecile. I hope to persuade her to tell you before you have to trek all the way to their capital."

Beside me, Prince Matthias tensed up.

I frowned. "Is there any other information that you know?"

The king stepped away and turned his head to the wall behind him. "Just look at this tapestry. Do you notice anything strange?"

I studied the city of Erabyn and the castle above it, but found nothing strange until I focused on the sun. "The shadows are long."

"What was that?" asked the king.

"The sun is at its peak, but the shadows are long," I repeated, my eyebrows furrowed in concentration.

The king smiled once again. "Correct. Come closer." I stood and made my way around the desk. "Anything else?" he said.

My gaze immediately fastened back onto the sun, and I spotted something red stitched into the fabric. I looked closer. "A phoenix," I said. Sewn in thin maroon thread was the fire bird, its wings outstretched and its mouth open as if it itself was creating the fiery orb surrounding it.

"This tapestry is portraying a time when darkness is covering the land, but also a time when the sun—and the phoenix—are at their highest. You represent hope for our kingdom in a time of shadows."

"Is darkness overshadowing the kingdom right now?" I asked.

"You tell me," he said. "More and more of my soldiers disappear each day, and the rulers of Onwin and Kislow are saying the same thing to me in their letters. Ginsey and Pira are killing them."

I raised my eyebrows, surprised that he didn't know the truth. "You're wrong."

The king scrutinized me, a warning look in his eye. "I'm wrong?"

I nodded. "King Ciaran's numbers are growing every day. He's stealing your men."

The king's grip tightened on the back of the chair in front of him and he narrowed his eyes. "My men would never do such a thing."

"I thought you would already know what's happening to them," I said.

He crossed his arms. "And what's that?"

"He's controlling them with blood magic."

It took a moment for him to process the information. When he had, he sat heavily in his chair, his dark eyes flitting out the window. "If you're right, Ivy...then the prophecy must be upon us. King Ciaran will destroy us all, with Pira as their ally."

"Pira?" I asked.

The king nodded. "Pira has always been an ally of Ginsey. If Ginsey fights, Pira will join—"

"You have to be the phoenix of prophecy, Ivy," cut in Prince Matthias, his gray eyes boring into my own. "You could save us all."

King Giddon suddenly rose out of his chair and walked over to a shelf stacked with scrolls. He reached up and took one from the top shelf. Then, he came back to the desk and set it in front of me. "Which is why I've decided to make you a Leviathan noble."

The document in front of me was a map, and circled was a city in the mainland, just south of Erabyn.

King Giddon placed his finger on the city. "That's where your new home will be. You will be Lady Ivy of the Brinestone Estate."

Chapter Fourteen

I STARED AT the king, speechless. Finally, I managed to say, "Is—is that even possible? I thought you had to be born into nobility."

"Of course it is," he replied, his jaw clenched stubbornly. "I have absolute rule over this kingdom. You are the phoenix, the probable savior of my people. If I want you to be a lady, you'll be a lady."

"But—"

"I will not change my mind," the king said firmly. "The ceremony is to be held two days from now. I'll have the best seamstresses in Erabyn see after your dress." With a dismissive gesture, he said, "Matthias, show her to her rooms. We'll continue our talk of the prophecy soon."

The prince stood and held out his arm. I stared at the king as he began to sort through the papers on his desk, but he didn't look back up. In a daze, I took Prince Matthias's arm. He led me to the door, unlocked it, and then stepped outside. As soon as the door was shut, I withdrew my hand from his arm. "You have to find some way to stop this. I can't be a lady."

He narrowed his eyes as he began to walk back the way we'd come. "Is there something wrong with having power and a name for yourself?" He paused for a moment, as if to gather his thoughts. "What about all the money that you could distribute to the poor? Or all the orphans you could house on such an enormous estate?"

I glanced at him out of the corner of my eye, reluctant to show that he'd struck a chord with his manipulation. "I have a problem with the extra responsibility of owning the property and the servants. It just...doesn't sit well with me."

The prince frowned. "You're going to have to get used to it. You don't want my father as an enemy."

I held in a laugh. "He would consider me an enemy if I refused his gift?"

His looked away. "In a manner of speaking."

We stopped beside a white, arched door that stood out between two tapestries.

"This is it," Matthias said as he opened it for me.

I went past him into the large room. All the furnishings were white, like the door. A four poster bed was draped with a light blue bedspread, and the tall windows were framed with elegant curtains of the same color.

The prince spoke up from behind me. "My father knows what's best for the kingdom."

I turned to face him with pursed lips and no reply.

He took a step back, eyes stormy. "You'll see."

I stared at the place where he'd stood, at the stained glass that depicted a ship sailing on fair seas. *Thrown into nobility unwillingly? This is definitely not what I expected when I left the conservatory.*

I stepped forward to close the door, but was stopped short when a woman appeared in the doorway. Her breath came in short bursts as if she'd hurried to get there.

She wore a white gossamer gown that had a lace collar and long, flowing sleeves. Her eyes were pale periwinkle and her white-blonde hair was braided and twisted into a bun.

After a while, the surprise passed and unease settled in. "Can I help you?"

She snorted, causing her beauty to fade in my eyes. "You speak like a servant girl." Her voice was thick with a strange accent I'd never heard before. She stepped in the room and looked me up and down. "You are the one they call the phoenix, yes?"

I crossed my arms. "Yes."

She circled me. "You need to eat more. A twig isn't likely to save anyone."

I narrowed my eyes. "Did you just come here to insult me? Because if that's the case, I invite you to leave."

She gave me a condescending smile. "I came to check under the bed. My servants forgot to bring something of mine."

I frowned with the realization that I was speaking to Princess Cecile of Onwin. I watched silently as she crossed to the other side of the room, and lifted the dust ruffle. "Ah," she said, pulling out a wooden bin. "Here it is."

I looked at it with one raised eyebrow. "Couldn't you have sent a servant to retrieve that?"

She shrugged. "I could have…but then I wouldn't be able to convey my message."

I braced myself. "And what is that?"

She ambled forward until our faces were inches apart. "Stay away from Prince Matthias. The only way Onwin and Leviatha will ever be able to form a lasting alliance is if the two of us marry."

I restrained a laugh of surprise. "Rest assured that I have no intention of pursuing a romance with your prince."

From the other side of the room, a loud voice rang out, dissolving the tension. "I do hope we aren't interrupting something."

Princess Cecile and I took a step back from each other and turned to face the person who had spoken. It was a rather large woman, tall and wide with broad shoulders and thick fingers. She was outfitted in a gaudy indigo dress with gold embroidery on the hem and a golden bodice. Although it is unkind to laugh at one's clothing choices, she made it extremely hard not to.

"Dame Guthrie," Princess Cecile said as she smoothed back a stray hair. "I was just welcoming Ivy to the palace."

Dame Guthrie gurgled out a laugh. At least, I thought it was a laugh. "If I truly believed that, I would remind you that you only arrived three days ago."

Princess Cecile pursed her lips. "And then I would reply that you should watch your tongue. I'm still above your rank."

Dame Guthrie stepped forward, a challenge in her eye. "Maybe if we were in Onwin, Princess."

The princess's grip tightened on her wooden bin. "Good day, Guthrie," she said as she walked past the large woman and out the door.

The woman didn't bother to curtsy as she passed. She turned and studied me. "Hmm. You are a slight thing, aren't you?"

I made no effort to reply, and she didn't ask for one.

"My assistants should be here shortly," she said. "But while they're gone, tell me… Did you really save the prince and his personal guard from a raging fire?"

"Uh…yes," I answered, surprised by her question.

She smiled widely. "Then your dress shall be the most beautiful piece of work I have ever made."

Hopefully, her definition of beauty ranged far from what she herself was wearing.

She turned on her heal as her assistants came into the room, carrying armloads of supplies. "There you are," she said as they dropped everything on the ground.

Dame Guthrie walked toward one of the doorways. "Not in there, you two. In here," she chided.

The two assistants took in a deep breath simultaneously, bent down, and began to pick everything back up. I started to help them, but Dame Guthrie peeked her head around the corner and said, "Lady Ivy, leave them to it, please."

I obeyed her, but didn't feel right about it.

The next room, I realized, was a closet as big as the bedroom adjacent to it, with a large floor-length mirror covering the entire back wall. The shelves and rungs were completely bare.

"Ah, the beauty of an empty closet," said Dame Guthrie. "So many possibilities for the clothes that will come to fill it."

She hefted a sigh. "Of course, you won't be here long enough for me to make you more than one or two dresses."

"How will you manage to make one in only two days?" I questioned.

"Nimble fingers," she said as she raised one of her pudgy hands. "And assistants, of course. Your gown is my first priority."

"How long have you known?"

Her forehead wrinkled as she thought. "Oh, about two weeks now? Something like that... Anyway, it was enough time to draw up a few designs while the prince went to get you."

So this was the plan all along...

Dame Guthrie's assistants pushed past me to set her things at her feet. "You know what to do," she said.

Without complaint, they both got straight to work. I imagine that if they *did* complain, their fate would be a whole lot worse with a woman like Dame Guthrie in charge of it.

When a platform was set up in front of the mirror, the heavy seamstress took me by the arm and pulled me toward it. "Up where I can see you."

The girl handed her a tape measure. Guthrie took it and began making her measurements.

I did whatever she told me, feeling like a puppet as the puppeteer pulled the strings.

She set out some fabrics for me to choose from, and soon found out that my favorite color was light green. "Interesting. It does bring out your eyes."

An hour later, when the session was finally over, Dame Guthrie gave me a kiss on both cheeks and said her goodbyes.

I slumped into a chair and stared out at the ocean, glad that I'd been given a room facing it. The sun was just starting to set and the orange light danced off the rippling waves hypnotically. My eyes drifted closed for a few moments until another knock sounded at the door. I jerked out of my stupor, confused at the sudden darkness outside. I'd fallen asleep.

The knock rang out louder and the door opened without my consent. "Ivy?" I looked back to see Sir Lochlan. "Why didn't you answer the door?"

"You have a habit of knocking while I'm asleep," I replied drowsily as I stood.

He walked over and held an envelope out. "This is for you."

I took it from his hands. The only name on it was my own. "Who is it from?" I asked as I broke the dark green seal.

"I have my suspicions, but I know for certain it's from Ginsey."

"Ginsey?" I looked closer at the seal, noticing for the first time the elaborate G stamped into the wax.

He nodded. "And I'd prefer to be here when you read it."

I bit my lip as I pulled out the folded paper and opened it.

Dear Ivy,

By the time you read this letter, King Giddon will have already made the proposition of making you a lady. How do I know that, you may ask?

I have eyes everywhere.

I'm watching you, Ivy, and I don't need a silly necklace for that.

When you choose to join my ranks, my gates are always open to you, and your friend, the griffin, will be released immediately.

But if you don't…let's just say there's only so much agony the human body can take.

It's your choice.

Cordially,

Ciaran A. Gregson,
King of Ginsey,
Head of the Saints of Sorcery

Chapter Fifteen

I DROPPED THE letter as if it had burned me. I didn't want to lay a finger on the same piece of paper that that man had touched.

"How did it get here?" I asked.

Sir Lochlan didn't open his mouth to reply until he'd picked up the letter and read through it. "There was a messenger wearing the Ginsian crest. King Ciaran wanted us to know that he sent you a letter." He paused to look down at the piece of paper in his hand. "I'm going to have to give this to the king."

I nodded. "I understand. Does he know that King Ciaran has spies here?"

Worry lines etched into his forehead. "Yes, but I don't know if we'll ever find out just how many of our men have joined his ranks."

I looked out into the dark night, remembering the circle of robed figures that had surrounded Kurt and me in King Ciaran's dungeon. "Have you ever heard of the Saints of Sorcery?"

He held up the letter. "This is the first time I've heard them called that, but I have heard of them. They're the ones that Roland talked about—who took over his mind."

I nodded. "The same ones that tried to take over me, too."

Darkness passed over his features as he creased the letter and slipped it back into the envelope. "You can never go back there."

My lips formed into a grim line. "I never want to." *But I have to.*

Sir Lochlan started back toward the open door, but paused before he shut it. "Try not to make many friends... We never know who among us could be one of them."

Later that night, a servant brought me dinner. Everything was prepared perfectly and set out on trays under metal lids. The bread was crunchy on the outside and soft and warm on the inside. The roast was tender and juicy. The vegetables were not too firm or too overcooked. It was delicious, but it was wasted on me.

I could only think of the letter. *He found out about the pendant.*

My only consolation was that the matching one was buried miles upon miles away and that King Ciaran still wanted Kurt alive. But how much longer would that last?

While I was sitting here, eating a perfect dinner, in a perfect room, with no threats to my life, Kurt could be screaming in pain as the whip was brought down again and again, our own father gathering his blood on the bristles of a paint brush.

My sleep was not sound.

Early the next morning, a maid came in to wake me up.

She shook my shoulder. "We have to get you ready, milady. The king has requested that you come to breakfast."

I was reluctant to get out of bed and face the day, but I forced myself to swing my feet to the ground.

The woman walked to the other side of the room and opened the door for two more servants to come in, one carrying a satchel and the other holding something wrapped in brown parchment paper.

"What are those?" I asked.

The girl carrying the satchel opened it up for me to see the contents. There were soaps and brushes and perfumes and makeup. I'd never worn makeup in my life, and I certainly didn't want to start now.

"I don't actually have to put that on, do I?" I asked, pointing to the various powders and inks.

"It's our job to make you look your best," said the head maid. "You're about to meet the rest of the royal family, after all."

I sighed and pointed to the thing wrapped in parchment. "And what's that?"

The servant girl handed it to me. "A gift from Dame Guthrie," she said.

I unwrapped the parchment and pulled out a sky blue dress and a pair of white heels.

"She said she was certain that they would fit you."

I held the dress up and let the rest of the fabric fall to the ground so that I could study the whole thing. I was relieved to see that it looked nothing like Dame Guthrie's dress last night. It was a simple design, but pretty.

The maids drew up a bath and then ushered me into the bathroom. After bathing, I wrapped myself in a plush white robe and opened the door only to be pushed into a chair in front of the mirror. The head maid approached me with scissors.

I studied them apprehensively. "What are those for?"

"Your hair, of course," she said as she brushed through the tangles. "I'm only taking a little off."

Before I could protest, the snipping started, and I watched out of the corner of my eye as hair fell to the ground. In only minutes, she was done and my hair was three inches shorter. Then, she began to style it as one of the younger maids began to apply powders to my face.

"Is that really necessary?" I asked, leaning my head away from the makeup brush she was using.

"Yes. Now hold still."

The last maid finished taking care of the mess in the bathroom and started trimming and filing my nails.

About thirty minutes and lots of poking and prodding later, they declared me ready.

They pushed me toward the closet. *Do I dare look in the mirror?*

Reluctantly, I did and stared in awe. My face was free of blemishes, my mouth looked fuller, my cheekbones sharper, and my eyes bigger.

"You look striking, milady," said the head maid, smiling at her handiwork.

I frowned. The person in the mirror was beautiful, but it wasn't me. It didn't fit.

"There's only three minutes before breakfast begins," she said as she hurried me to the door. "Do you know where the dining room is?"

"Um...I don't think so," I answered.

"I'll take you there, then."

She led me down a hallway, back toward the entrance of the castle until we got to a pair of closed double doors.

I opened one, giving way to sounds of forks against plates and chatter. My eyes had to adjust to the brightness of the room before I could focus on finding a seat.

The king sat at the head of the table, with a son on either side of him. Studying them, it was hard to tell which one was Prince Matthias and which one was his brother. They both had the same close-cropped sandy hair.

A woman sat at the side of one of the brothers, and Alyss and Grix sat across from each other at the end of the table. The only seat left was the one beside the last prince, and I assumed it was Matthias, judging by the way he watched me as I walked toward him. I wished that my hair were down so I could hide behind it.

King Giddon didn't even look up. "A little late, Ivy," he rumbled through a mouth of food. "I'm glad you could join us."

I knew it wasn't the best of manners to talk with food in your mouth, but I supposed for the king, it didn't matter.

"I trust that you slept well?" Prince Matthias asked.

"Yes, thank you," I said as I sat down and picked up a fork.

The king finished chewing and swallowed. "Now that we're all here, maybe we can discuss the rest of our plans. To briefly cover what you missed, Ivy, I've decided to let Grix and Alyss train with my soldiers for the time being. I see that my cousin, Drake, might have been a little…overzealous in his ways of punishment."

I looked up in surprise, nearly dropping the fork. "Headmaster Drake is your cousin?"

The king took a sip of his drink and sat back in his chair. "Yes, unfortunately. On my mother's side. Her sister married a trial wizard, and Drake was the result. I was never really close to her side of the family, but Drake became a soldier and climbed rank so quickly that I was forced to recognize him. He was the one that came up with the idea of a school for rare second forms. Before that, all of you just floundered out there in the world, without an appointed job."

Is that such a bad thing? I thought to myself.

"Enough about him, though. Let's talk about the plans I have for you."

I nodded for him to continue as I pushed scrambled eggs around on my plate.

"Today, your skills will be evaluated."

I accidentally let my fork clatter to the table, sending egg flying in all directions. My face burned. "Evaluated?" I asked.

"We already have obstacles set up for you in the Erabyn arena," explained the king. "We're going to see just how talented you are."

"When was this decided?" I asked woodenly, reaching for my fork again.

"Long before you came. But I decided last night that it would happen today."

I nodded and took a bite of egg that refused to go down. I had to swallow it with a few sips of water.

The king gestured to the son on the other side of the table. "Have you met my son, Prince Edwin yet? Or his wife, Princess Clara?"

"No, I haven't," I said as I put the cup down and smiled at them politely. "It's nice to meet you both."

"Likewise," said Prince Edwin.

Princess Clara, whose brown hair was braided over her shoulder, only gave a nod before her blue eyes flicked away.

Now that I took the time to study them, I saw that Prince Edwin had a little more weight on him than Prince Matthias.

He gave me a half smile, but like his wife, he wouldn't look me directly in the eye.

"Princess Cecile was going to join us, but this morning she said she'd taken ill and preferred to stay in her room," King Giddon continued.

"A shame," said Princess Clara. "She's a great conversationalist."

I picked over my plate until everyone else had set their forks down.

An uncomfortable silence settled over the room until the king stood and set his napkin on his plate. "We'll all continue to the arena at around two. Ivy, I'll have someone escort you there early so that you can get your bearings before it starts."

Then, he left. I could feel everyone's eyes on me, as I backed the chair from the table and said, "Excuse me."

I pushed through the door into the hallway. To the right, I saw the back of the king as he turned the corner. I found it hard not to be annoyed by this man that suddenly wanted to control my every action, but I kept my face blank as a servant passed me by.

I hurried to the left, in the direction of my room. It wasn't long before I heard quiet footsteps behind me. It could have been a servant, but something told me that wasn't the case. I turned around quickly to surprise the follower, relieved to see that it was only Alyss.

I waited for her to catch up.

"Is your room this way too?" I asked when she was only a few feet away.

She shook her head and looked up and down the hall before saying softly, "I have something I want to talk to you about. In your room."

"What is it?" I asked, lowering my voice to match her volume.

"Something about the king," she said, so quietly that I could barely hear.

With my curiosity piqued, we continued until we reached my door. It was open with the three maids still cleaning up.

"I'll finish that for you," I said as I entered. "You can leave now."

The three maids looked at each other as if they had been affronted.

"As you wish," said the head maid.

Each of them walked past with their head down, and the last shut the door behind them.

I turned to Alyss. "What was it that you wanted to tell me?"

She took a deep breath and walked a little further into the room before turning back, wringing her hands. "Well...I think the king is planning something."

"Something more than the obstacle course?" I asked, eyebrows raised. "How do you know?"

She shrugged. "I just get this...feeling with people. And Prince Edwin and Princess Clara were friendly and talkative before you got there, but then they went strangely silent when you came in the room."

I thought about it for a moment. "Wouldn't that just be because of the evaluation?"

Her eyes darkened. "It could be, but...I have a strong feeling that it isn't."

I sat on the edge of my bed. "What do you think he's planning?"

She looked away. "I don't exactly know. I just wanted to tell you in case something happens."

I picked at a loose thread on my dress, deep in thought. "I'll make sure to keep an eye out for anything suspicious."

She nodded and headed for the door.

"Alyss?" I said before she shut it. She peeked her head back in. "Thank you for telling me."

She smiled and closed the door.

Chapter Sixteen

At HALF-PAST ONE, Sir Lochlan came to retrieve me. As we walked, he glanced over and asked, "How are you settling in?"

"What's the point of settling in if I'm going to leave in a few days?"

His gaze returned to the floor. "True… Are you ready for the challenge?"

Another surprising question. Why did he care? "I can't be ready for something I don't know anything about."

"One thing I can tell you—the arena will be overflowing. It usually is when the king holds a challenge."

"Does he do it often?" I asked.

"Maybe once or twice a year. I got to give some input on the obstacles this time."

"Oh, really?" I stole a look. "Did you take it easy on me?"

His mouth broke into a secretive smile. "Not in the slightest."

After emerging from the castle into the bright sunlight, he led me up to a carriage and helped me inside before settling in across from me. He knocked on the ceiling and we heard a *hyah!* and the crack of a whip as the horses were spurred forward.

I gazed out the window as we neared the docks. The ship we'd come in on was still there, with not a soul on it. Around the palace gates, there were guards, but only a few villagers gathered along the road. "It's strange to see it so empty out there. They know the king is coming, don't they?"

"There will be more soon," he answered, resting his head against the wall.

It didn't take long to see that he was right. Many people were walking by the road even before we hit Erabyn. Some waved at the carriage as we passed.

Erabyn was a strange city. Unlike Achron or Redrune, even the heart had wide, open streets and buildings spaced far apart. The closer we got to the arena—which appeared to be a smaller, round replica of King Giddon's castle—the more people clogged the road ahead of us.

Ahead, the gates opened, and crowds began to pour in. I heard the carriage driver shouting, "Make way!" as he slowed the horses to a walk.

We entered in those same gates and skirted around the side of the building until we were at the back, where a single black door stood, dwarfed by the sandstone wall.

Sir Lochlan pushed the carriage door open, stepped down, and held it for me. "Quickly," he ordered.

I climbed down and he slammed the door shut behind me, ushering me toward the black door. It opened into total darkness.

"The servants must not have gotten back here to light the lanterns yet," he remarked.

"I guess not," I said, squinting. Slowly, my eyes adjusted to the darkness enough to see faint, flickering light bending around the curved tunnel.

We walked toward it, soon finding two servants who worked quickly to light the way.

"This should have been done half an hour ago," Sir Lochlan grumbled as we approached.

The younger servant blanched while the older man bowed and said, "I'm very sorry, sir. This was unexpected."

"Hurry up and get them lit before the king shows up."

"Yes, sir," he replied as he turned back to his work.

We continued until the tunnel split into two separate paths, one to the right, going up a set of stairs, and one to the left, going down. We went left and walked on until Sir Lochlan turned into a giant arched opening in the wall. I peered through, but my eyes searched in vain. There was nothing to see except black emptiness, everywhere.

"What is this?" I whispered.

"The cage," Sir Lochlan replied. "It's formed by wizards. To everyone outside, the walls aren't even here, and the darkness seems like gray fog. They will be able to see everything, even when you can't. These illusions will be able to hurt you, so don't slack off in combat."

Why do all trials have to involve wizards? "How long is this going to take?" I asked.

"It won't stop until you're broken," was all he said in reply.

"Broken?" I asked as I turned to him.

All I saw was his retreating silhouette, outlined by the torchlight in the tunnel. "It starts in ten minutes. I suggest familiarizing yourself with your surroundings."

My heart quickened when a black wall materialized where he had gone, pitching me into total darkness. I stretched out my hand as I walked forward, trying to feel for the wall. As soon as my flesh met the liquefied shadow, it seemed to take hold of me. Before I knew it, it was crawling up my hand, reaching for my arm. I jerked back, but it held fast.

With all my might, I pulled until I tumbled to the ground.

Though the hand that had touched the wall was completely numb, my other hand felt the cool grass I'd fallen on. Grass that I was certain hadn't been there before. As I pushed myself up, the room became brighter until I gazed upward at a full moon and stars, shining through a meadow that continued to grow taller around me. The dark corners in the sky were the only things left that hadn't been taken over by the illusion.

I got to my feet as the growth of the grass slowed to a stop and a few dead trees pulled themselves into existence beyond the field. Eyeing the trees warily, I started forward. I found a large tree and pushed my back up against it until I heard a small voice that must have come from outside the cage.

"Settle down, everyone! The trial will start in about a minute."

Fear clenched my stomach, cold and bleak, as I counted down the seconds.

Fifty-nine, fifty-eight, fifty-seven, fifty-six…

Three.

Two.

One.

The low sound of a horn echoed through the cage, but…nothing changed.

Then, I heard them. Footsteps coming up behind me, silent as the whispers of grass. Quickly, I unsheathed my sword and struck. Blade met flesh and a scream pierced the air, ricocheting off the walls of the cage as the body of a black panther melted into the earth.

I looked up to meet several pairs of glowing eyes. Wolves, cougars, lions, tigers, hyenas. All warrior forms. They snarled as they closed in on me.

A lion with a thick black mane got to me first. I struck at him, but he dodged to the side and lunged forward, tearing through fabric and skin. I narrowed my eyes as I pushed him off with a growl.

The sword got in the way. This would have to be a test of might.

I threw my sword to the ground and bent my knees, hands held at the ready.

Through the walls of the box, I could hear the faint sound of a laughing crowd.

The lion lunged again, thunder rumbling from his throat, but this time, I caught his front leg with my hands and swung him into the line of enemies. His body crushed two wolves. While their broken remains sunk down into the earth, the giant cat got up again, limping, his lip curled in a fierce snarl.

The tears on my shoulder and hands throbbed as they started repairing themselves.

I didn't hear the crowd laughing anymore.

I was anticipating his next move when all the warriors began to shift into their human forms. While their bodies and features looked normal, their eyes were pupil-less and void of emotion. I reached down and grabbed my sword's hilt, waiting for someone to strike.

The man that had shifted from the lion acted first. He swung his ax at me, but I dodged the blow and easily sent the tip of my sword through his heart. When I slid it back out, there was no red, no dripping blood. The man sunk to the ground and melted just like the two wolves and the panther had.

They're not real, I repeated in my mind as I focused on the rest of my enemies. *Illusions.*

More closed in on me, but my fear was ebbing. I broke into full attack mode, hacking through armor and flesh, melting all the warriors down into the earth like wax until only one female warrior remained.

We clashed blades together in a volley of movements. Within seconds, my blade slid into her stomach. She stared at me with gray pupil-less eyes, and to my horror, began to speak. "You think you're finished," she said in a monotone voice, "but I have more brothers and sisters. They're coming for you."

I jerked the blade out and the woman sunk into the earth. As soon as she was gone, warriors appeared throughout the field, too numerous for me to count. Unlike the last ones who were slow to attack, these ran at me, weapons drawn. I narrowed my eyes and shifted into the phoenix, hefting myself into the air with a stroke so strong that the first line of attackers was blown back.

I dodged spears and arrows that were aimed to ground me. *The grass is dry. The trees are dead.*

It was obviously the wizards' intention for me to set the entire cage aflame. So I did.

I swooped downward, flame erupting from my beak as I drenched the warriors in fire. The grass caught easily and began to spread. Within minutes, the blaze stretched high and hot, consuming everyone until the last fighter fell to the ground.

My heartbeat jolted in my chest when a sudden explosion of light lit the sky accompanied by an earsplitting clap of thunder. My ears rang as rain poured from the sky and my fire sizzled into smoke. The storm got stronger and stronger until the wind seemed to gust from the ceiling, working with gravity to push me to the ground.

Except there was no ground. Instead, I was plunged into the tossing waves of an ocean.

I tried to make my way to the surface, but the swirling current held me captive until I was dizzy with the lack of air. As a last resort, I shifted back into first form, and kicked as hard as I could. Finally, I broke through, flailing and spitting up sea water.

I gasped in a few breaths before realizing that the rain and wind had stopped. The choppy waves stilled into a gentle roll, and the clouds cleared away to expose a blue sky. The sun beat down on me as I floundered in the middle of the ocean.

I spun around in circles, waiting for something to appear above the waves, but there was nothing. No pirate ship, no land in the distance. And then, something touched my foot. Something big.

I yelped and shifted into the phoenix as fast as possible, flapping my wings clumsily and somehow managing to get into the air.

I studied the seemingly endless ocean, waiting for the enemy to make an appearance. Then, a row of copper-colored spines broke through the surface and slithered back into the waves.

A sea serpent. Just like Roland. I remembered that Sir Lochlan said he had helped plan out the obstacles, but if he'd helped with this, it was going too far.

The serpent resurfaced, one brown eye staring at me. And then it lunged. I dodged out of the way just in time. His teeth snapped the air where I'd been flying moments before.

He plunged back into the water as I circled around, not wanting to hit the wall of the cage. I was still tilted to the side when the sea serpent struck again, too fast for me to dodge. It clamped down on my wing and started to sink back into the water. I shrieked in pain and blasted the serpent with a ball of white-hot fire. He let go with an angry roar and dove back into the water. I tried to keep my wing from collapsing under the pain, but I'd taken too much damage. I spiraled into the briny ocean, wincing as salt invaded my wounds.

I opened my eyes underwater even though it stung. *What now?*

Desperate, I shifted into half-form and unsheathed my sword awkwardly.

I jumped when movement flickered beside me and struck at it as hard as I could. My blade pierced through scales, and it seemed as if the entire ocean trembled with the roar of the serpent. It lashed its tail at me, and suddenly, I was up in the air once again, arms and legs thrashing. When I came back down, I hit a hard surface. A cold surface.

I hit ice.

The blow knocked the breath out of my lungs and I gasped with the effort to get it back. As soon as I was able, I pushed myself to my feet unsteadily. The entire ocean had frozen into a white, choppy wasteland. I fully expected the sea serpent to break through and swallow me whole, but to my horror, a voice spoke up from behind me instead.

"It's been a while, Ivy. A few weeks, perhaps?"

Dread filling my heart, I turned around to find a dripping Roland, the water that splashed onto the ice mingling with blood that pooled from his stomach. He held my sword in his hand.

"Roland." In my mind, I knew that it wasn't really him. This was just another nightmarish mirage. But for some reason, this one involved blood.

He came closer, twirling the sword in his hand, his eyes dark.

"Don't," I said, backing away. My foot slipped, and I collapsed onto the ice. Roland took the opportunity to rest the tip of my sword on my throat.

"This is the end, Ivy."

I narrowed my eyes as my mind whirred to find a solution. "No. It's not."

And at the same moment that he would have slashed down with the sword, I channeled fiery heat into the ice and plummeted down into the freezing water. I drifted in icy cold for a few moments before everything disappeared and I hit the floor of the arena, shivering uncontrollably. The crowd was silent. At the edge of the cage, three stone pedestals of wizards fought amongst themselves, some angry, others dazed.

"Ivy, come with us."

I looked back to see Grix and Sir Lochlan.

Fiery anger raged through me as I reached for a sword that wasn't there. "How could you?" I growled at Lochlan. I lunged for him, but Grix held me back. I knew I was strong enough to toss him away, but even in my anger, I didn't want to hurt him.

Instead, I fumed silently until the red cleared from my vision, and I saw the way Sir Lochlan almost trembled with rage, his face ashen.

"Do you think it wasn't painful to see my dead brother like that?" he demanded, eyes blinking rapidly. "Do you think I would dishonor him in such a way?" The muscle in his temple pulsed as he clenched his jaw. "There's an enemy among us. Perhaps a team of them."

Grix pushed me back by the shoulders and looked into my eyes. "We need to get to safety. Now."

Chapter Seventeen

Sir Lochlan, Grix, and I hurried out of the arena, forgoing the carriage to travel with the swifter alternative— horseback.

Sir Lochlan led us down a steep hill, away from the raucous crowd, and kicked his horse into a gallop when he reached the field below. Grix and I raced after him, but he'd set a hard pace. Pretty soon, the horses beneath us snorted and panted with the effort.

After we crested the highest hill, the road and the front gate came into view. The guards opened it for us without question, so either a messenger had been sent ahead or they recognized Sir Lochlan from afar.

We pushed our tired, sweating horses past the wrought iron opening, slowing only once we reached the front doors, where we dismounted and passed the reigns on to a stable hand. Grix and Sir Lochlan hurried up the steps.

I started to follow them, but stopped when the stable hand asked, "What's the rush?"

I turned and shielded my eyes from the sun this time so that I could study his face. "Ayon?"

He flashed white teeth in a smile. "Surprised?"

"How did you get here so fast? I thought the wedding—"

"Ivy!" Sir Lochlan interrupted from the door. "We need to get inside!"

I gave Ayon an apologetic glance as I continued up the steps. "I'm sorry. We'll have to talk later."

"Oh... That's fine," said Ayon, but his smile had turned into a frown as he looked up at Sir Lochlan.

I hurried up the steps and through the door, which Sir Lochlan shut behind me.

"I advise you to stay in the castle until all of this is over. And I'll be appointing guards to stay at your door every day," he said

I twisted toward him sharply. "You know how I feel about guards."

He wouldn't look at me. "You have no say. Grix will be your day guard, and I'll think about it some more before I decide who I trust enough to be your night guard."

I bent my head to stare at my feet. If I had to have guards, at least Grix was one of them.

When we reached my door, Sir Lochlan continued walking past it. "Keep watch outside while she cleans up, Grix," he called over his shoulder. "The king will probably send a messenger as soon as he gets back."

"Yes, sir," Grix replied as I entered my room.

Once I was through, he shut the door behind me, leaving me completely alone. I sighed and walked to the washbasin, where a pitcher had been set.

After washing up, I sat on my bed and waited for the king's messenger to come. When the minutes started to drag by, I grew restless. To occupy my mind, I began to shuffle through the drawers of my nightstand. I almost shut the first empty drawer when something caught my eye. In the very back, a small piece of parchment was folded up and shoved into a crevice. I pulled it out and unfolded it, smoothing down the wrinkles. It read:

Dearest Cecile,

My heart grows colder each day I am forced to go without seeing your beautiful face.

You move with the grace of a gazelle. Your eyes are the color of twilight clouds. Your lips are like springtime blossoms, full and perfectly pink. I look forward to the day when I can meet those lips with my own.

Please visit soon, or I may be have to forget my duties here just to be by your side.

Yours forever and always,
Matthias

I was torn between laughing at the lovesick letter and heaving up the lunch that was sent to my room before we left for the arena. Princess Cecile must have meant for me to find Prince Matthias's message. She thought that I meant to replace her.

Not in a million years.

A knock sounded on the door, startling me from my thoughts. The king's messenger.

I set the letter down on the nightstand, and hurried to open the door to find not the messenger, but the king himself. As soon as I had the door open, he pushed past me. "Lady Ivy, I hope you'll forgive my intrusion," he said as he closed the door behind himself. "But we have important matters to discuss." He clasped his hands behind his back. "I've decided that your stay here should be extended."

I narrowed my eyebrows. "Extended? Is this because of the attack at the arena?"

"Not exactly," he answered. "But I've been thinking about this for a long time, waiting for this day to come."

I raised an eyebrow. "Waiting for what?"

He hesitated, looking past me out the window. "Ivy, I find you to be a fascinating creature. You have the rawest power that I've ever seen in a shifter, let alone in a female…"

I waited for him to continue, clueless to where he was going.

"You see, tomorrow will not be a mere ceremony. It will be your wedding."

My entire world spun to a stop. "W-what do you mean? Wedding?"

He placed his hand on my back and guided me over to the sitting area. "I'll explain myself to you. The royal line is weakening. I was the only one that survived of my siblings, and my boys were the only ones that survived out of the eight that my wife bore over the years. The six that died were healthy babes, but not one of them lived past the age of two in the end. Matthias and Edwin got sick often as children, but when they grew into men, they were strong. Strong enough to hide it when their bodies succumbed to sickness again."

I shook my head and backed away, fighting off the urge to clamp my hands over my ears.

"You see, you may be right where you need to be. Right in the place where you're needed most. To marry Matthias and strengthen the royal line in our time of need, when the shadows are longest and the sun is at its peak."

I shook my head. "No. That can't be my purpose."

"Maybe you have multiple purposes," the king rumbled. "This sacrifice will save your kingdom from eventual ruin. You *are* on Leviatha's side, aren't you?

I sat there, stunned for a moment before I stood and walked to the nightstand, where the letter still lay, unfolded. "Why don't you explain this?"

The king took the letter out of my hand and began to read it. By the end, he was chuckling and shaking his head. "This does not sound like Matthias at all. In fact, it rather sounds like Prince Edwin's writing style. But, if this is indeed something that Matthias sent on purpose, it was probably when he was very sick. He may have wanted a pretty little hand to hold on his deathbed."

I cringed. I certainly didn't want to be that pretty little hand.

I shook my head. "I'm sorry, Your Majesty, but I'm afraid you've asked the wrong girl to be the wife of your son. I'm simply not cut out for—"

"Nonsense," he said in a severe tone, narrowing his eyes. "I didn't ask." He took a step forward and stuck a thick, calloused finger in my face. "This is your duty, and you *will* do it. To strengthen the royal line and to save your kingdom from ruin."

"But—"

He waved his hand away and clenched his jaw. "I will hear no more about it. Matthias is on his way now to talk and plan with us."

Sure enough, not three seconds later, a knock came at the door.

The king had his mouth open, ready to scold some more, but snapped it shut to answer the knock instead. Prince Matthias walked through, avoiding my gaze.

"About time," said King Giddon. "Let's all sit down." Prince Matthias followed his father back to the sitting area. *Maybe I should run,* I thought, eyeing the door longingly. In the end, I trailed reluctantly after the prince.

"The wedding will be tomorrow, at the exact time that the ceremony to make you a lady was planned," the king began. "That way, we haven't wasted good money and food on a celebration that never happens."

"I can't—"

The king cut me off with a look.

"I'll have our best event planners on the job, and of course, I already told Dame Guthrie to include a lot of white in the dress design."

By the sound of it, it was never his plan to make me a lady. Just a princess. And Dame Guthrie had known.

"You knew that this would be a wedding," I accused.

The king shrugged. "Maybe. I'm glad you proved yourself powerful enough to gain the role of princess, soon to be queen, and mother of future kings."

He continued on into his planning. "We'll inform the closest noblemen and women around to see if they can make it. I know it will be very short notice, so there shouldn't be much of a crowd." The king continued on and on until the words just faded into the background. I felt dizzy and rested my head on my palm to calm the sensation.

I was brought out of my stupor when a boot came into view, and then a knee. I looked up to find Prince Matthias kneeling in front of me, a ring with several small diamonds pinched between his thumb and forefinger. "Ivy...will you do me the honor of becoming my bride?"

This was the second proposal this year, and it felt just as unexpected and unpleasant as the first, if not more so. I prayed that I wouldn't throw up. I shook my head once, but one look at the king behind him made me reconsider. There was a warning in his eyes, and I knew that I would be in danger if I said no.

Instead, I looked back down and said, "It's too soon. I can't marry you so soon."

Prince Matthias paused and looked back at his father. The king sighed heavily. "Then you have one week," he conceded.

The prince looked back at me as he slid the ring on my finger and glanced up with shadowed gray eyes. Underneath his stare and the king's, I finally cracked. I gave a slight nod. "Okay," I whispered.

Prince Matthias didn't smile as he stood. He leaned forward awkwardly and gave me a peck on the cheek while holding my hands. I looked over Prince Matthias's shoulder at that moment to see the king's smug smile. He gave me an approving nod, and it was all I could do to hold on to my lunch.

When Matthias finally backed away, the king patted his back and led him out of the room. The door clicked shut behind them, leaving my mind reeling.

What just happened? What have I done?

Chapter Eighteen

I WAITED A few minutes after the prince and the king had left, and then followed them out the door. Grix looked around in surprise.

"What was all that about?" he asked.

I glanced down the hallway, making sure King Giddon and his son were nowhere in sight. Seeing no one, I turned back to Grix. "I'm engaged to Prince Matthias."

His eyebrows shot up, and for a moment, his mouth opened and closed like a fish. "How was that decided?" he finally got out.

I pinched the bridge of my nose. "It was all a blur. I was pressured into it."

Confusion clouded his features. "But…why?"

I was about to answer, but a servant rounded the corner at the end of the hallway. I stepped back into the room and waved for Grix to follow.

Safe behind the door, I continued. "The king told me that the royal line was weakening. He believes that part of the prophecy is about saving the Leviathan kingdom by bearing his son's children."

Grix rubbed his stubbly chin. "When is the wedding supposed to happen?"

"In a week," I said, dread seeping into my voice.

"A week?!" Grix said loudly. I looked at the door, hoping no one heard. Grix lowered his voice. "Just a week?"

"It was going to be tomorrow."

"That's not right. A week is far too short of a time to plan a wedding, let alone a single day. Why must it be so soon?"

I shrugged. "I have no idea…but it doesn't matter. I won't be here."

His eyes widened. "You mean you're going to—"

"Run. Like I always do," I finished for him.

"The king will send men after you. He'll search far and wide until he gets you back. Are you sure you want to chance that rather than refusing the offer directly?"

"Of course I don't want to," I retorted. "But it wasn't exactly an offer. I tried to say no. The king forced me."

Grix ran a hand through his hair. "Well, at least you've got a few days to make an escape plan."

"And to say goodbye," I added.

Grix shook his head. "Not to everyone. If you're leaving, Alyss and I will come with you. We already decided we would."

"No," I said firmly. "I need you both to stay here. I don't want you to be in trouble because of me, not to mention I'll be able to cover more ground on my own."

Grix paused to think about it. "What about King Ciaran's men? Aren't they searching for you, too?"

"They'll have a tough time catching up with me in the air."

Grix frowned, eyebrows pulled down into a line. "Are you sure?"

"I am."

He gave a nod. "When will you leave?"

I paused to think about it. "Maybe the day after tomorrow. I want enough time to say goodbye, while sparing the servants unnecessary work."

"That sounds about right," he said. "You will be missed."

We both swiveled to the door when a sudden knock rang through the room. Grix glanced at me, and then stepped forward to answer it.

"Alyss," he said, in obvious relief. He pulled her in and shut the door.

She looked at me, eyes wide. "I heard the news. This must be what the king had been planning."

"It seems that it was," I replied.

"I'm so sorry. I only wish I had known…"

"How could you? Unless you're capable of reading minds."

She gave me a thin smile. "If only I could."

I stepped toward the door. "I'm going to let Grix explain everything to you. There's someone I need to see."

"Wait," Grix said. "I have to come with you."

I paused with my hand on the doorknob. "Stand outside the door as if you're still guarding me. If I'm caught, I'll tell them I escaped from my window."

Grix looked uncertain. "I don't know—" he said, but before he could protest further, I was already out the door and halfway down the hall.

When I rounded the corner, a crowd came into view, all gathered around a man who read words off a piece of parchment. My feet faltered.

"The royal wedding is in a week's time," he said over the noise of the crowd. "All servants are expected to help in the setting up of the ceremony and the dinner afterward, in one way or another."

Everyone seemed confused.

"Didn't she just get here?"

"A commoner princess!"

"Only a week?"

They were so absorbed in their conversations that I was sure I could get away...until I felt a hand on my shoulder.

"Did you think you would sneak off without anyone noticing?"

At just the sound of his voice, my shoulders lost their tension. I turned to Ayon, and smiled with relief. "Thank goodness it's you."

He didn't reply, but instead looked at the crowd and pushed me forward gently. "I think we need to talk."

"That's why I was headed to the stables," I replied as he led the way out. "I wanted to find you."

After descending several steps, Ayon stopped and turned to me, eyebrows shadowing his deep blue eyes. "Is all of that true? You're going to marry the prince?"

I looked around. Along with the guards stationed at the door, there were also a few people wandering along the gravel path. I kept my voice down to make sure no one heard. "I had no choice," I finally answered. "The king wouldn't take anything other than a yes."

He clenched his jaw. "Is that what I should have done? Bullied you until you said yes?" He winced after the words came out.

Even though I knew he regretted saying them, they still stung.

I tightened my hands into fists, and hissed, "No, it's not. Because I'm leaving."

"Leaving? To go where?"

I shrugged. "Onwin, I guess. That's where I'll learn the entire prophecy. I'll learn what my destiny really is instead of what King Giddon thinks it is."

"What are you saying? Destiny?"

"There's a prophecy written about a phoenix," I explained. "Everyone seems to think I'm that phoenix."

He rubbed his forehead, eyes pressed closed. "I'm supposed to believe that there's a prophecy about you?" He looked up. "I grew up with you, Ivy. I've known you since you were a little girl, and now you're supposed to save the world?"

I couldn't hold back a smile. "You're the first one to think about it like I do."

A sad look passed over his face as he dropped his hand back down to his side. "I just wish things were back the way they were before all this happened."

"Believe me, I do too," I replied.

We paused when the door behind us opened and a handful of servants came out, deep in conversation. When they saw me, they lowered their voices, but I could still hear them.

"Is that her?" one whispered.

"I think so," replied the other. "I heard she had red hair like that and green eyes."

Even after they'd descended the steps, they kept shooting looks at me.

"I don't envy you," Ayon said after they'd gone. "If the entire kingdom wasn't talking about you before, they certainly are now."

"Great," I said under my breath. I leaned against the wall, and shook my head, ready for a change of subject. "How's Emillia?"

"She's settling in. It'll be an adjustment to get used to castle life."

I nodded. "When did you get here? I expected it to be a lot longer before your arrival."

He shoved his hands into his coat pockets and shrugged. "As soon as I got back to Emillia with the news, we saw no reason to delay the wedding any further than the next morning. Neither of us know many people and we couldn't afford a big, fancy wedding anyway. I promised my mother I would visit and then we left." He gestured up to the castle with a jerk of his head. "And now we're here."

"Did Emillia handle all the traveling well?"

"She's surprisingly a good traveler. Being a horse, I was our main transportation. I carried us each day as long and as fast as I could. Didn't want to get caught by bandits, you know?"

Like the ones I'd run into.

He continued. "Luckily, the only trouble we had was pulling together enough money to afford a ship to get to each island, and eventually, the mainland."

"Looks like you did a pretty good job."

He smiled. "Mother lent me some money. Anyway, what about you? Anything happen after I left?"

I opened my mouth to reply just as the door opened again. Princess Cecile stepped out, seemingly in deep thought. She didn't even look up from the ground until she was only a few feet away.

She paused for a moment, her face pleasant at first. Then, her mouth pinched into a frown and her eyes darkened in anger. "You," she hissed.

She glanced at Ayon and struggled to smooth over her features again. She plastered on a fake smile and said, "Lady Ivy, would you accompany me to my quarters?" Then, without another word, she started back up the steps.

I don't know why I did it—perhaps because of curiosity— but I gave Ayon a nod and followed the princess back through the door.

We skirted around the few remaining servants in the hall and turned a corner. Her door was the first on the right, painted red. She turned the handle and stepped inside, her purple-ish eyes glinting as she waited for me to follow her.

Hesitantly, I did, but I never turned my back on her as she shut the door behind us.

With the door closed, she rounded on me. "What are you thinking? Didn't I tell you that the prince and I are the only way Onwin and Leviatha can form an alliance?"

I crossed my arms. "I was under the impression that our kingdoms were already allied. Is Onwin planning on joining sides with Ginsey now?"

She glared at me. "We'd rather side with Ginsey than be obliterated by them."

I let her steep in her anger for a moment before I said, "You'll be happy to hear that I'm not going to go through with the wedding."

Her face morphed from angry to surprised to disbelieving. "What do you mean? I thought—"

"King Giddon forced me into the betrothal. So I'm going to run away the day after tomorrow."

She lifted her delicate eyebrows. "Run? Where?"

"To Onwin, I guess. I'm tired of hearing about a prophecy I still don't know."

She stared at me for a moment. "Really?"

I nodded.

She played with her sleeve, her face screwed up in concentration. "You'll have a hard time getting into the Black Fortress... I'll have to come with you."

"I can't be slowed down—"

"My second form is a swan. We'll be able to fly out of here in the middle of the night and get about a seven or eight hour head start. Even Leviatha's best flyers won't be able to catch up before we cross the border."

I raised my eyebrows. "What about your mission to marry the prince?"

"That can wait until his father stops obsessing about you," she said. "If the king doesn't like our union, it won't happen."

"Should we meet somewhere?"

"The palace gate. Midnight. Don't be late."

I nodded and stepped toward the door, but she caught my wrist as I reached for the handle.

"This better not be some joke," she said, her eyes narrowed.

I pulled out of her grasp, cold dislike coiling in my stomach. "Believe me. It's not."

Chapter Nineteen

THE FOLLOWING MORNING, King Giddon brought me to the ballroom to meet various decorators and event planners. Initially, I thought I would have to interact with them, as most brides would do for their wedding, but King Giddon took control of the situation. Mostly, I stifled yawns, pretended to listen, and tried not to squirm in the hard-backed chair.

Apparently, Prince Matthias wasn't required to attend. I wrestled back my jealousy as the seconds ticked on.

"Lady Ivy?"

I looked up, caught by surprise.

"Your favorite flower?" prompted one of the decorators.

"Um…" I wasn't exactly certain, but I thought back on the last memory I had of my mother. Of the fire flower she'd put in my hair. "Which ones have red, yellow, and orange, like a fire?"

"There are many kinds, but you may be thinking of Blazeblossom."

I nodded my head. "Right. That one."

The king hefted a sigh and sat back in his throne. "She can have that in her bouquet, but I truly insist on using roses throughout the room."

I pursed my lips. *Calm down, Ivy. There won't be a wedding anyway.*

I waited in silence as the rest of the meeting dragged on.

When it was finished, Grix, who had stood by my side during the entire meeting, escorted me out of the room behind the king. I was relieved when he turned the opposite direction of my room.

"So…" I said once Grix and I were out of earshot. "How are you doing?"

He snorted, shaking his head. "I feel like I know more about wedding planning than I do fighting right now."

My laugh rang through the hall. "You're not alone."

I was in surprisingly good spirits as we continued on, but when Sir Lochlan rounded the corner followed by Prince Matthias, my smile faded.

"Ivy," Matthias said as he stopped in front of me, his gray eyes taking me in. "How are you?"

I shrugged and pasted on a fake smile. "Good, I guess. What about you?"

"Overwhelmed, as I'm sure you are," he answered.

I nodded and shifted my feet as silence stretched on.

The prince bowed his head, his mouth pressed into a thin line. "Well, I'll leave you to…whatever you're doing. If I don't see you beforehand, I suppose I'll see you at the betrothal dinner tomorrow night."

"Betrothal dinner?" I asked.

He tilted his head. "Didn't Father tell you about the dinner?"

"He may have, but I must not have been listening." If the dinner lasted too long, it could delay the plans to escape.

"It's just a formality. A few noblemen and women will be attending, but nothing huge," he said.

I struggled to keep my face from falling. *Why do nobles have to have so many meetings and dinners?*

Matthias stepped to the side. "Until then."

I glanced at Sir Lochlan, who dipped his head and followed the prince, avoiding my gaze. Normally, he was cold and put together, but today, I thought I saw a flicker of guilt in his eyes.

Had Lochlan known the king's plan?

❖   ❖   ❖

The rest of the day was pleasant. I was left to my own devices, except when Dame Guthrie came to give me the dress for the betrothal dinner. She fluttered around me like a plump peacock in her purple and green monstrosity of a gown, repeating how excited she was for the wedding. Knowing she'd already been told to make my wedding dress before she had me fitted, it was hard to be polite in her presence. I was relieved that she didn't stay long.

Grix and Alyss were able to eat lunch and dinner with me. We read books, played card games at the table, and relaxed until Grix's shift was over. He'd just stood up to leave when three loud raps came at the door.

Grix cracked the door open to look out, and upon seeing the visitor, swung it open the rest of the way, enough for me to see Sir Lochlan and another guard.

I stood. "Yes?"

"Ivy," Sir Lochlan said as he led the other guard in. "This is your new night guard, Jake."

The name sounded familiar. I studied the man. He was older than Sir Lochlan and had the beginning of crow's feet around his eyes. His hair was already balding, though it kept its dark brown color.

Then, it hit me. "Your brother?"

He nodded. "And the only other person I trust to keep you safe."

I swallowed around the lump in my throat. "Did you tell him—?"

"He knows everything," Sir Lochlan said.

Jake held his hands behind his back. "It is a tragedy that the youngest and brightest of our siblings is no longer with us, but I know that isn't your fault. I will gladly serve my future queen."

Guilt coursed through me. *I'll never be anyone's queen.* But I forced my mouth into a smile. "Thank you, Jake."

He gave me a grim nod and turned to go back out the door.

"Sir Lochlan," I called just before he followed after his brother.

Lochlan turned back and raised his eyebrows.

I glanced at Alyss, who'd already stood and was making her way out the door. I don't know how she could tell, but she threw me a look that told me she knew I needed a private conversation. She grabbed Grix's hand as if it were the most natural thing in the world to do and led him out the door behind her.

I looked back at Sir Lochlan.

He stood stock still, hands by his sides. "What is it?"

"Had you known?" I whispered.

"Known?" he asked, but his countenance betrayed him. He knew what I was talking about.

I crossed my arms and waited for him to explain.

He turned his head toward the window, hazel eyes so like Roland's now that his expression softened. "Yes. I'd known."

"And that's probably why you hated it when I ran off," I concluded.

He wouldn't look at me. "The king told me before we left that my mission was to get you down here, even if I had to tie you to the top of the carriage to do so."

I winced. "That's a bit harsh."

Sir Lochlan glanced nervously at the door, where his brother stood with his back toward us. "He can be that way."

"And the prince knew, too?" I asked.

"He knew," Lochlan said as he looked back at me. "He took the softer approach."

I stared at him silently. Although he may feel guilty, telling him my plan to run again would most likely get me caught. He was too loyal to the royal family, despite their faults.

"Thank you for telling me," I finally said.

He nodded sharply and fixed his face back into an emotionless mask. He stepped out of the room and closed the door behind him.

That night, I tossed and turned, too busy thinking about what could be happening just twenty-four hours later. Knowing I would need it, I willed myself to sleep, only to be met with nightmares. In one, I wore a wedding dress, but the veil clouded my vision. When it was lifted back, I found not the prince standing as my groom, but King Giddon.

The thought kept me shuddering throughout the next day until my maids came in to get me ready for the dinner at only four o'clock. I'd just finished lunch less than three hours before.

However, I have to admit, it was nicer than the previous time, when they'd hurried frantically through every step. I didn't particularly like being made up, but at least I got to relish the time I had before dinner.

As always, Grix was my escort when the time came to leave my room. The maids laid the make-up on thick and teased my hair up into an absurdly high bun. By the end, I wished I could stick my head in a bucket.

The dress Dame Guthrie had left for me wasn't much better. It was all white with silver beading, but the skirt poofed out and the sleeves wrapped around my arms too tightly.

The fact that Grix stifled a laugh when he saw me didn't make me feel much better.

"Oh, laugh it up," I said, rolling my eyes. "I'll never feel more ridiculous than I do right now."

He shook his head with a grin. "You don't look ridiculous. You just look nothing like Ivy."

When the open ballroom doors came into view, I cringed at the crowd gathered around them. At first, they continued on with their conversation, but as more and more people became aware of my presence, the talk quieted down. Some people stared openly and others were satisfied with little glances. I slowed to a stop, unsure of what to do until I saw the prince waving me over to where he stood next to Sir Lochlan.

"Ivy, I don't think you've met Lochlan's fiancée, Celia, have you?" he asked as I approached. The woman he gestured to was tall and strongly built under her armor, and though her face was heavily freckled under short black hair, she still had an unusual beauty about her.

I was slightly perturbed by her stature compared to mine, but I managed to say, "No, I haven't. It's nice to finally meet you."

She dipped her head into a slight bow. "The pleasure is mine."

Sir Lochlan looked past me into the ballroom. "As soon as the king finishes talking with the duke and duchess, we should be able to get inside."

I followed his gaze, and now that there wasn't a door blocking the way, I could see the king's bright face as he talked to an older couple. As we watched, the duke bowed his head and the king gave a nod before they continued into the room.

Like Sir Lochlan said, the crowd diminished quickly after the duke and duchess were through, and we inched forward with everyone else until it was our turn to be greeted by the king.

"Ivy, Matthias, welcome," he said, not even taking into account Grix, Sir Lochlan, or Celia. "Your table is on the platform." He pointed to a small table, raised higher than all the others.

As we continued on through the ballroom, I asked Prince Matthias, "Are we expected to sit at that table alone?"

He nodded. "Yes. Our guards will sit at a nearby table."

I cringed inwardly. "And the king, your brother, and his wife?"

"They'll sit at the table next to us."

The placement seemed a little odd to me as we climbed up the stairs. "Is this usually how betrothal dinners work?"

The prince shook his head. "I don't think so. I haven't gone to many betrothal dinners, but I think my father had it positioned like this so we could focus on each other."

I sat down in the chair uncomfortably, feeling every eye in the room on me. Prince Matthias took the seat next to me. All we had left to do was wait until the festivities started.

I jumped when a servant came up behind me with a pitcher to fill my cup.

Prince Matthias chuckled and took my hand. "Nervous?"

I squeezed out a dry laugh. "Maybe a little." I itched to pull my hand away, but with so many eyes on us, I knew I needed to *try* to act like the prince's betrothed.

When everyone had gotten to their places, the king made his way up from the door and climbed up on the platform behind us. I craned my neck around to see him, but Matthias tugged on my fingers, indicating with his eyes that I should keep facing straight ahead.

I turned back to the people below me uneasily.

"In honor of the soon-to-be Princess Ivy—" He paused as he placed a necklace of white flowers over my head. "—and my son, Prince Matthias—" I watched out of the corner of my eye as he did the same to the prince. "—we feast!"

As soon as he said the words, all the side doors opened and servants poured in, carrying endless trays of food. It seemed like half of them were headed toward us. The table began to fill up, dish after dish.

I stared at everything, overwhelmed. "Any more food and the table would collapse."

The prince chuckled. "That's how my father likes it." He let go of my hand to reach forward and help himself to a platter of sliced roast beef, shoveling it onto his plate before moving on to the next thing and the next. I followed his lead, though I didn't pile my plate too high, knowing that I didn't want to be sick while running away.

"Good idea," prince Matthias said as I picked up my fork. "Save room for dessert."

I smiled. "That's my plan."

As I lifted a forkful of mashed potatoes to my mouth, my gaze fell down to the crowd below. I immediately picked out Princess Cecile. She sat at the same table as the duke and duchess, and as if she could feel me looking at her, her eyes met mine. She gave a nod and continued her conversation with the duchess.

I picked at the food for three hours before the guests started leaving. Most of them came up to us with their congratulations, while others had clearly only come for the meal.

"Can we leave yet?" I asked Prince Matthias quietly after a particularly drawn out conversation he'd had with a lord.

He shook his head. "It's polite for a host to stay longer than the guests, unless they're absurdly late in leaving or drunk."

I sat back in my chair, though I was careful not to slouch since I was still acting proper.

Matthias smiled at me knowingly. "Maybe I can take you on a walk through the courtyard afterward?" he suggested.

"Maybe," I said noncommittedly as I pushed the dessert plate away from myself, wishing I had eaten less.

A servant came up to clear my place and something about her ringlets of honey-blond hair and her thin mouth seemed familiar. When she glanced at me, her dark brown eyes gave her away.

"Emillia?" I asked.

Her lips flickered into a smile. "I'm glad to see that you remember me, milady."

"Of course I do. I was hoping I would get to see you."

She hefted up my dirty dishes and one of the platters of picked over food. "I plan on being here for a long time," she said, glancing at the prince. "I'm sure you'll see me in the halls every now and then."

"Right," I said, hoping I hadn't given myself away. I wondered if Ayon had told her that I was leaving.

"Old friend?" Prince Matthias asked after she slipped away.

"More like acquaintance," I answered. "And Ayon's new wife."

He squinted his eyes and looked up at the ceiling. "Is that the fellow that came to be a stable-hand?"

I nodded and watched as the duke and duchess stood up to leave. The duke looked up at the prince and me and gave a bow. Prince Matthias answered the gesture with a respectful nod.

When the couple left, it seemed like that was the key to the end of the dinner. Most everyone followed them in the next few minutes, Princess Cecile among them. I watched her as she left, thinking of our plan.

"Ready to go?" the prince asked as he stood.

He helped me down the steps of the platform, and when Grix and Sir Lochlan came to escort us the prince held up his hand. "I'd like a moment with Ivy. You are dismissed for now."

I silently begged for Grix not to go anywhere, to stay with me, but he could only give me an encouraging half-smile and nod of goodbye as he turned away.

Chapter Twenty

PRINCE MATTHIAS HELD out his arm as he led the way into the hall. I hesitated in taking it, but knew that I had to. I didn't want to give any inclination that I didn't intend to follow through with the wedding plans. I reached for his arm, but it was already too late for him not to notice a hint of reluctance.

The more distance that passed between Grix and me, the more endangered I felt until finally, we turned the corner and were out of sight. Matthias led the way through a side door, into a courtyard. I shivered at the chill. The light of the sun had faded into dark gray, but lanterns lit up our path. I had been trying to keep a few inches between me and the prince, but to my dismay, he pulled me closer to him.

I sighed. At least he was warm.

He gazed down at me. "Ivy, our wedding day is getting closer, but I feel like we've only grown farther apart since getting off the ship."

I wasn't sure what to say and found it hard to look him in the eye.

He guided us forward until we stood in front of one of the fountains. "I think we would both benefit from spending more time together before standing at the altar."

I decided to go along with it. "You're right," I said. "I'd rather not marry a complete stranger."

He raised an eyebrow. "But I'm not a *complete* stranger. We've known each other for..." he paused to think.

"About two weeks," I said, an eyebrow raised.

He lifted his shoulders. "And that's not bad. I've known plenty of nobles with arranged marriages who only got to see their betrothed once before the wedding."

I shuddered. *At least I haven't been subjected to that.*

I struggled to find the right words to say. "I'm...grateful to have more time." Without the time, it would've been a lot harder to get away.

Prince Matthias didn't say anything. Without warning, he reached under my chin and tilted my head up. The lantern behind him gave him a golden outline, but his face was shadowed. And then suddenly, his lips were pressed against mine.

It seemed as if time stood still for a moment. I was frozen, my mind spinning, scrambling to figure out what to do in this foreign situation.

I went with my first instinct, and shoved him away, momentarily forgetting that I had unnatural strength. What I thought was going to be a little push sent Prince Matthias tumbling back into the fountain with a splash. A few droplets landed on my burning face. I could only watch as he came up for air, choking and gasping, legs still caught on the ledge.

With wide eyes, I hurried forward. "I'm so sorry. I didn't mean to—"

His shoulders started to shake as he plunked each foot into the water and attempted to stand. I thought he was shivering at first, but then realized it was laughter.

"I guess you weren't ready for that, huh?" he finally managed to say, his short hair sticking up in odd angles.

"I guess not," I said, biting my lip to keep from smiling. When that wasn't enough, I put a hand to my mouth to stifle the giggles that threatened to escape. Instead, I just ended up snorting, which sent us both into a fit of laughter—something I'd thought impossible with this particular person.

When the laughter finally died down, I realized he actually *was* shivering and his lips had turned a pale blue. Worry settled in. "We have to get you inside."

The king had said that Matthias and his brother were prone to illness, and while I certainly didn't want to marry the prince, I didn't want him sick either.

He didn't protest when I took his arm and dragged him back inside the way we'd come. The halls weren't much warmer than the outdoors, so I led the way to the closest fireplace…which just happened to be in my room. Jake stood at attention as soon as we rounded the corner, but he had to take a second glance when he saw the soggy prince.

"Is everything alright?" he asked, eyebrows shooting upward.

"I got pushed into a fountain," said Prince Matthias, smoothing back his hair.

"By accident," I added, shooting the prince a look.

With a slow, calculating nod, Jake shifted away from the door and faced forward.

Just before I took the prince inside, I remembered the pack that I'd left on one of the chairs. If the prince got curious enough to look through it, it could terminate my escape plan. I turned, trying to stay calm. "Can you wait here for just a moment?" I asked. "I need to check to see if I left anything out while getting ready." I blushed, berating myself inwardly at my carelessness.

He knitted his eyebrows, blue lips trembling. "Okay…but h-hurry."

I pushed inside. Before I shut the door, I heard Matthias giving Jake orders to bring him another uniform from his closet.

I hurried across the room and grabbed the pack, shoving it under the bed. I was about to go get the prince when I saw movement out of the corner of my eye. When I glanced over, I was startled to see a big white bird sitting outside the window, graceful neck turned toward me. Princess Cecile. She pecked on the glass once, staring at me with hard eyes. I was torn between helping the prince and opening the window to let the princess in. In the end, I hurried forward and pushed it open. Cecile dropped inside, flapping her wings at me angrily.

"Stop," I whispered. "Prince Matthias is just outside the door."

The swan tossed its head and began to shift form. As soon as Princess Cecile had her human mouth back, she hissed, "You were supposed to meet me outside the palace gates thirty minutes ago!"

I gestured wildly at the door. "I was kind of busy trying not to blow our cover. Prince Matthias wanted to take me on a walk through the courtyard."

She hefted a sigh. "You could have feigned exhaustion."

"None of that matters now. You have to go," I said, trying to push her back out the window.

She resisted. "I will not. It's freezing out there! And I've already sent my servant ahead with a note to my father."

There was a rap at the door. "Just a minute!" I shouted. "Go, go," I whispered, pushing the stubborn princess toward the closet.

As soon as the door was shut, I hurried to the fireplace. "You can come in now," I shouted as I tossed a couple logs on the flickering coals.

"You must not keep a very clean room," said Matthias as he opened the door and shut it behind him. He made his way over to the fireplace, dripping water all over the rug.

"I guess not," I replied tightly. I threw on another log for good measure, and closed my eyes as I focused on strengthening the fire. Before long, the flame grew from a few flickers into a roaring blaze.

"That should be good," Prince Matthias said.

I opened my eyes and backed away to let him take my place. Soon, the water rose off his clothes in steam.

"Shouldn't you get a little further away?" I asked. "I don't want the fire to burn you."

He shrugged. "It feels good for now."

There was a knock on the door, and Jake entered with an armful of dry clothes. "I hurried as fast as I could," he said as handed the uniform over.

"Where should I—" began Prince Matthias.

"The bathroom," I said immediately, gesturing to the door. "There should be a towel in there too."

As soon as the prince had the door shut behind him, Jake stepped back out into the hallway, leaving me alone and awkward as I tried to calm my nerves.

I jumped when the bathroom door opened, and the prince stepped out in dry clothes, his others wrapped in one of my towels. "I'm afraid I'll have to take this one," he said, lifting it. "I'll make sure it gets replaced."

"Oh, don't worry about it," I replied. "I'll just ask my maids to fetch me a new one in the morning."

"Whatever suits you," he said as he went back over to the fire. I noticed that his shivering had come to a halt.

Trying to give a hint, I stretched and yawned loudly.

Luckily, he wasn't completely senseless. "Right. It is pretty late."

I followed him as he made his way to the door.

"I suppose I'll see you tomorrow?" Matthias asked with a glance back at me.

"Tomorrow," I replied, watching as he turned in the direction of his room.

I closed the door and put my ear against the wood until I heard his footsteps die off. With a sigh of relief, I hurried to the closet and opened it to find Princess Cecile smirking at me. "Took you lovebirds long enough," she said as she pushed past.

She strolled over to the window as I reached under the bed for my bag.

"Ready to be a runaway bride?" she asked.

"Ready," I said as I looped the bag around my neck and shifted into the phoenix.

Chapter Twenty-one

As the sun rose higher on the horizon, I could only imagine what my maids would think when they found an empty bed and an open window. Hopefully, they'd assume I'd woken up early and gone on a flight, but it wouldn't take much longer to figure out I'd run away. And Princess Cecile's simultaneous disappearance would tell the king exactly where we were headed.

The afternoon sun beat down from the sky when the princess couldn't go any longer. We coasted down into the long grass that seemed to stretch forever in all directions. The princess could barely stand after she'd shifted form, so I offered to keep first watch.

I looked over at Princess Cecile, who hummed in her sleep for the hundredth time. She looked a lot different when her face was peaceful instead of pinched.

I'd let her use my pack as a pillow while I sat uncomfortably on a nearby rock, listening for sounds of intruders. The last hour was the hardest, with the clouds above stained orange with sunset and the crickets warming up for their nightly symphony. I fought through the fatigue until it was finally Cecile's turn to take over.

When night fell, we flew over the remainder of the Leviathan plains until we reached a foreboding stone wall, lit up for miles with thousands of torches. A black and yellow flag flew high in the air above an outpost, the white shape of a hawk sewn in the center. We'd finally reached safety…or so I thought.

As soon as we crossed into the new kingdom, a roar sounded. Soldiers filed out of the building onto the wall, pointing loaded longbows at us.

My heartbeat raced in my chest.

The source of the roar was a large black panther, its eyes glowing in the torchlight, its tail flicking back and forth as it watched us. Princess Cecile seemed unruffled as she circled over them.

I followed her lead, even though it was difficult to stay calm with weapons aimed at us. We circled five times before the soldiers lowered their weapons.

The black cat shifted into a man and waved us down.

Princess Cecile dove down to the wall and landed on the walk as she changed form. I was right behind her, shifting almost as fast.

Each person on the wall immediately dropped into bows except for the man that had shifted from the black cat. "Back to your posts," he barked behind him. Most of the soldiers looked like they'd rather stay and eavesdrop, but they did as their commander ordered.

The man bowed his head slightly in greeting as he said, "Your Grace. Your servant said that you'd be coming this way shortly."

Her eyes flashed with anger. "Yes. I sent her ahead to make sure we weren't threatened by your archers."

He regarded her tone with coolness. "Since you've been gone, princess, we've been getting more and more attacks from every side of our wall. We're losing men every day. This is protocol for all who wish to cross our border. Even you."

This news of the attacks silenced Cecile and gave the man the chance to turn his attention on me. "The servant girl didn't tell me you were coming. Running away, are we?"

I was speechless. I'd hoped that the news hadn't spread this far, but clearly, it had. Before I could fumble for a reply, Princess Cecile spoke up. "These attacks on our kingdom prove that she's doing the right thing. Her destiny is to save all the kingdoms, not just Leviatha through marriage."

The man scrutinized me silently. "Be on your way, then," he finally said. "Leviatha will be the third kingdom at our throats, but if you think it right, Princess, then so be it." He turned away, and headed back toward the garrison.

Princess Cecile turned to me for the first time since shifting and looked up at the sky. "We'll land in Furling Gap in the morning. My home is just a day away from there." She looked down and raised her eyebrows. "Ready?"

We shifted form simultaneously and took off into the night.

Furling Gap was a small village located in the bottom of a shallow ravine where, even in the colder days, the grass still grew greener. We spent the day at an inn, relying on locked doors and windows while we got our fill of sleep. When we awoke, we ate a quick meal and resumed our travels.

Only a couple hours after leaving, a bolt of lighting flashed ahead of us, among big billowing clouds that shadowed the dark sky. I circled back to Cecile to see if she had seen what I'd seen, and from the look in her eye, she had.

We flew low over the grassy hills. As the clouds neared, so did the cold winds, and it wasn't long before the sleet pelted our wings. Below, I spotted a big barn and headed straight toward it, flying through the open window into a pile of straw. Princess Cecile followed my lead, and then we were watching out the window in human form as we ate what was left of the bread I'd brought from the inn.

"Thanks," Princess Cecile said after we'd finished eating. "I wasn't sure how much longer I could hold on."

I raised my eyebrows, surprised that she'd actually said something nice. "No problem." I brought my knees to my chest and tried to rub the chill from my arms. "How much longer is it until we reach the castle?"

"Five hours, as long as we don't have to stop again," she answered.

We sat quietly until the sleet turned into a misty drizzle. Then, deciding to take the chance, we shifted into our second forms and flew back out into the night.

I could see the lights of the castle when the wind kicked back up and rain started to pour again. Since this was Princess Cecile's territory, I hung back to let her lead the way.

The fortress was shaped like a cube, with no towers except for a disconnected one built across a wide moat. In the dark, the castle walls looked like black concrete. Each window was barred with spiked iron, the same kind that surrounded the moat in a tall, foreboding fence. Princess Cecile made her way to the tower, seemingly the only entrance and exit from the fortress, at least from this side. She landed and shifted form where the light didn't reach, so I did the same.

Then, slowly, she walked forward into the light, clothes and hair dripping with rainwater.

"WHO'S THERE?!" someone boomed through the roar of the storm.

"Princess Cecile Vierra!" she shouted back. "And a friend!"

After a moment of silence, the door at the bottom of the tower opened and two guards came out, carrying lanterns. They raised them to our faces, and upon seeing that Cecile was truly who she claimed to be, they bowed. "Allow us to accompany you inside."

She nodded. "Thank you."

As soon as we were back in the tower, one of the guards approached a ladder and yelled up, "Lower the bridge for the princess!"

As we waited for the bridge to come down, Princess Cecile said, "Did my servant come to tell you of my arrival?"

The guard shook his head. "No, this was quite a surprise, milady."

She looked at me, the corners of her mouth pulled down in worry. "In that case, I'll need someone to notify my father of my arrival. He'll want to know."

"Are you sure you want to risk waking him up?" the guard asked.

"He wouldn't have it any other way."

He nodded and when the bridge clicked into place, we continued onward. Inside, the fortress was just as unwelcoming. The walls were gray and lined with the heads of animals and old weapons. Pelts littered the floor in a thick, multicolored carpet. Four large, muscled guards stood at attention as soon as we got through the doors, faces carefully blank.

I don't know what I was expecting, but this certainly wasn't it.

As if knowing what I was thinking, Princess Cecile raised an eyebrow. "What do you think?" she asked, waving her hand around.

"Intimidating," I answered truthfully.

She gave me a satisfied smile. "This is home."

It was hard to believe that someone as graceful and beautiful as Princess Cecile had been raised in a place like this.

"I can take it from here," she said to the guard. "Tell my father that I'm in my room when he's ready to see me."

The guard bowed his head in acknowledgement. I followed Princess Cecile through another door, into a hall with a high ceiling and white pillars, tinted gray by the lack of light. There were windows, but they were barred just like the ones I'd seen at the front of the building. Princess Cecile crossed through the pillars to get to a large door with spikes. It seemed like such a door should be locked, but the handle turned with no problem. Cold air blew out from inside. I peeked into the room, but could barely see anything.

"Excuse me, milady," came a voice from behind me. I stepped aside for a small servant girl who carried a bucket of kindling. She hurried inside, toward a fireplace that I could barely make out.

"Ivy will take care of the fire. You may go," Princess Cecile said to the girl. The girl gave a curtsy, and scurried out of the dark room into the lit hallway.

I went over to the fireplace, and began to arrange the wood. When I reached my hand forward to light the fire, I could feel Princess Cecile watching me closely. Within minutes, we had a roaring blaze.

She came closer for the warmth. "It is amazing that you can do that. In your human form, no less."

I turned to study the room. "The power isn't my own," I replied. The plant amplified whatever power God had given me.

Despite the spiked door, it was actually the first welcoming room I'd seen, though the walls were still gray as a gargoyle. There was a bed piled with pink pillows and an entire wall of drawn pictures. Separated by a few stairs, there was also a small library with a sitting area. I lit a lantern I'd found by the bed and carried it over to the wall to study each of the drawings.

"Oh, don't look at those," called Princess Cecile from the fire. "I thought I was an artist when I was a child, but most of them are absolutely horrible."

It was true, some of them were pretty bad—such as the scribbled one of someone holding what I assumed was a puppy…or a monkey…or a baby. But as I continued to walk along the wall, the drawings got more and more detailed until I reached the end, where she'd painted a picture of battle. She didn't leave anything out. There was lots of blood and the heart-wrenching faces of people in pain and people with bloodlust in their eyes and people who were sobbing. Even though I wanted to tear my eyes away from it, I couldn't.

I jumped when I heard her voice right beside me. "You're probably wondering why I would paint such a thing." Her eyes appeared haunted as she studied her own handiwork. "There are people who want war. There are foolish boys who say they're not afraid of it, that they could hold their own in a fight. But war isn't just a fight. There is blood and death everywhere. There is pain and dying screams. There are loved ones that you lose. War is horrifying."

I finally tore my eyes away from the painting when the door opened. I turned to see a short figure with a bald head and a full beard standing in the doorway. "Cecile?"

"Father," Princess Cecile said as she walked forward. When she reached him, she didn't hug him. She just stood there, her hands clasped together.

King Torran stood a full head shorter than his daughter. He was an odd looking man with thick black eyebrows and large ears. The only thing he and his daughter shared was the purplish eye color.

"What is the meaning of this?" he growled, the bridge of his nose wrinkled as he scowled at her. "You were supposed to—"

Her shoulders tensed. "I think you should know that I brought important company."

He seemed to notice me for the first time, and he raised an eyebrow. "Important company? More important than the prince of Leviatha?"

"Yes, actually," the princess said.

"Who is she, then?"

Princess Cecile stepped from between her father and me. "She's the one you've been waiting for. The phoenix."

King Torran stood in stunned silence…and then burst out laughing. "You stole her from Leviatha?" he asked with a gap-toothed grin.

"I didn't *steal* her," Princess Cecile said. "She didn't want to get married."

The king shook his head, suddenly serious once again as he looked at the ground. "This is going to threaten the peace with Leviatha," he said while stroking his beard. He lifted his head and smiled slightly, "But ever since I heard the phoenix had been discovered, I knew that it wouldn't be long before the fighting stopped."

"But how can I make it stop?" I asked, speaking in his presence for the first time.

His gaze flitted to Princess Cecile. "Have you told her anything?"

Princess Cecile shook her head. "What little I know is still secret."

"Good. Then we can start from scratch. Follow me," he ordered as he swept back into the hall. "It's time you both see what lies beneath the castle."

Chapter Twenty-two

As SOON AS we walked out of the bedroom, we were flanked by armored soldiers. It struck me as odd to be walking through the halls with a king when he was only wearing a robe, but that was overruled by the excitement of learning the prophecy. The excitement *and* the dread.

For the prophecy to be so famous, the task at hand must be nearly impossible.

Next to me, Princess Cecile seemed excited as well, but her eyes were tinted with something I couldn't quite place. *Jealousy?*

My attention was divided when we came to a halt beside what looked like a plain gray wall, no different than any other in the fortress. The king muttered incoherently to himself as he ran a hand over the stone.

"What?" Princess Cecile asked when I didn't have the nerve to speak up.

"It's been years and years. I can't remember which stones to press." He turned to his men with a determined scowl. "Bring the battering ram. We'll bring this wall down one way or another."

"What's on the other side?" I interrogated as the guards filed out.

"Patience," the king said. "It will only be a few more minutes, and then you'll know everything."

The king still stared at the wall, his eyes squinting as if he were still trying to remember how to get to the other side. Finally, the men came back, bringing more soldiers to help carry the heavy log.

King Torran pushed us back. "Hit the wall right where I was standing," he ordered his men.

The battering ram was maneuvered around to face the wall, and then the guard at the helm shouted, "Ready? Heave!"

The men drew back as far as they could and hurtled the beam into the wall. The entire palace shook, but the wall remained seemingly unharmed.

"Ready? Heave!" the man repeated, and they drove the battering ram into the wall again. Dust fell from the ceiling like snow drifts.

"Are you sure you can't remember how to open it?" I asked, afraid the roof was going to collapse on our heads.

The king didn't answer, instead choosing to keep his attention solely on the men who were ramming into the wall over and over again. People were beginning to gather at either end of the hallway, but the king waved them off when he saw them.

After about fifteen hits and no progress, the king muttered, "This isn't working," under his breath. He walked forward as they were readying themselves for another blow. "Stop, stop!" he yelled. "We need to try something else." He rubbed the back of his bald head, and then his eyes focused on me. "You, Ivy. Why don't you try something?"

Glad to have the ceiling still intact above my head, I stepped around the guards and studied the wall. Like the king had before, I rubbed a hand against the stone. When my skin touched the wall, it seemed to hum with energy as one of the stones lit up. I pressed my hand against the cold surface and the light faded as another stone above it lit up. This happened seven times before something like a click sounded and the wall began to rotate.

The king clapped his hands together as a dark tunnel appeared. "That's what I wanted to see," he said, that gap-toothed grin showing again. "Guards, stay here and make sure no one passes. This is something that we need to do alone."

The majority of the guards nodded, and after the king lifted a torch from the wall, Princess Cecile and I followed him down the hall.

"Why haven't you ever taken me down here?" Princess Cecile asked.

"Because when you were little, you were barely able to keep a secret." He brushed a cobweb out of his face and continued. "And when you were older, I had forgotten the code, as you just witnessed."

Before long, the tunnel siphoned out into a larger room, one just as empty as the tunnel before it. "There's nothing here," I said, gazing around the room.

"Don't give up hope just yet," the king replied.

He walked forward, and as soon as his foot hit the stone in the middle of the room, the ground under us began to shake. Princess Cecile and I cast a worried look at each other. "Is that supposed to happen?" she asked.

"Wouldn't I be running if it wasn't?" said the king.

I wanted to go back into the tunnel for shelter, but as soon as I turned back, the floor dropped. I crouched down on unsteady legs and placed a hand to the ground to keep my balance. Soon, the tunnel was out of sight, just another shadow in the darkness above. *If the battering ram didn't bring down the fortress, this sure will,* I thought.

Then, the rumbling stilled and the falling floor jolted to a stop. I pushed myself back to my feet and turned back toward the flickering torchlight.

"See? Not so bad," the king grumbled, but I could tell that the hand holding the torch was shaking.

"How are we going to get back up?" I asked.

"It should take us back," said the king, "but if it doesn't, we all have our wings. It shouldn't be too hard to find the tunnel somewhere up there."

On the other side of the room, another tunnel had opened. Princess Cecile and I followed King Torran once again.

At the end, the torchlight only expanded so much, and the echoing room around us was a black chasm. I couldn't see anything.

As I followed the king alongside the wall, I had to keep my focus on the floor. It was made of tile, but several times, I nearly tripped over fallen rocks that had crushed and cracked it.

"Somewhere here, there should be a…" He paused as he looked for it. "Ah, here it is!" He touched the torch to a groove that had been carved in the wall. It sizzled for a moment before the fire caught and began to spread. It swirled around the room, curving around the corners of the wall and illuminating the entire space.

Contrary to what I had believed, the room wasn't very big at all. The ceiling was high, but not nearly as high as the last room.

I studied the area. We were standing on a platform, and below, row upon row of golden sarcophagi lined the space.

"A tomb?" I asked, taking an involuntary step backward.

"How'd you guess?" was the king's sarcastic reply.

"No wonder I always thought the castle was haunted," Princess Cecile muttered.

The king abandoned the torch and walked toward the single sarcophagus that was raised on the platform with us. "The prophecy is over here."

As we picked our way through the rubble, I asked, "Are these your ancestors?"

He turned with a glint in his eye. "No. They're yours."

I steadied myself on the bannister. "My ancestors? What do you mean?"

He gestured to the engravings in the gold. "Take a look."

The writing was loopy and somewhat difficult to read in the dim light, but I eventually made it out.

It read:

The phoenixes have fallen,
their fiery forms reduced to ash.

Darkness has overtaken the land,

ruled by a dragon's hand.

But soon, another phoenix will come,

to slay the scaled beast.

What was divided into the five will become one,

when we rise again, bright as the sun,

to bring back a land of peace.

"That's it?" I asked. I felt like laughing. "I'm just supposed to slay a dragon?"

The king raised an eyebrow. "Do you think it will be easy? Do you know how big a dragon is?"

"How could I? I've never seen one."

"Neither have I, but I've studied them in books. They're rumored to be as big as this room and capable of burning down an entire village with one breath."

"It's a good thing I'm immune to fire," I said.

"Not dragon fire." He gestured down to the tombs. "Do you want know how most of these phoenixes died? They were reduced to ash when the dragon burned down the palace that once stood right where we're standing."

My relief lessened. "Then if this one dragon was capable of slaughtering an entire community of my kind, what makes me different?"

"You're immortal, aren't you?" Princess Cecile asked.

"Well…I don't know," I said, absent-mindedly tracing the scar over my heart. "I don't think so."

The king coughed, eyes bugging out of his head. "Wait a minute… Y-you mean to tell me that you consumed the plant of eternal life?"

"Not on purpose," I said.

"Well, what was it like?" he prompted.

"Painful," I said with a grimace.

He wrinkled his forehead. "Painful? How?"

I pulled aside my sleeve to expose the ugly, jagged scar that traced across my shoulder. "It gave me this."

He led me closer to the wall so he could study the scar in the flickering firelight. "Strange. From my studies, the plant was only supposed to give strength and immortality. I've never heard of something like this."

Princess Cecile stepped up next to her father, a look of worry on her face. "Should we take her to the healer?"

"Absolutely not," said the king, turning on his daughter. "We can't have just anyone knowing the secrets of the kingdom."

"But he's been the family healer since I was a baby," she argued.

"Still…" the king said. "I'm the only one that has studied the plant extensively. Unless you include Edibus Finch."

Princess Cecile screwed her face into a sour expression.

"Who's Edibus Finch?" I asked.

"My childhood tutor," the king replied. "Taught me everything I know."

"I guess we should pay old Edibus a visit, then," sighed the princess. "Great." The sarcasm was thick in her voice.

Curiosity got the better of me. "What's so bad about him?"

"He's just…hard to handle for long periods of time," she replied.

The king shook his head. "That's an understatement. Follow me."

He picked up his torch again and we started back through the tunnel. Once the middle stone was triggered, the floor began to rise again, but at a much slower pace. It felt like ages before we reached the main floor. When the shuddering came to a complete stop, the king set a brisk pace through the hallway and into the openness of the wide corridor, with the battering ram sitting on the floor and soldiers littered about. I was grateful for the morning light that poured in from the window, especially after being in that dreary tomb.

"If you would close the door, Ivy," the king said, gesturing to the wall.

I looked at it. *How?* Luckily, when I pressed my hand to the wall, it responded immediately by shifting back into place as if it had never moved at all.

"Clear the hall," the king ordered. "Back to your posts. You two, with me."

Two burly men fell into place beside us as we walked down the hall and up a flight of stairs. The air was warm, but stuffy. We continued through an empty servants' hall until we came to a humble door at the very end. Before anyone had the chance to knock, the door swung open and a man that resembled a bat peeked out.

He had pointed ears and a comb-over with long, greasy white hair. His spectacles were as thick as dessert plates and almost as large. "What's all the ruckus?" he grumbled in a raspy voice. "I wasn't alerted that a parade of elephants would come tromping down my hallway this morning."

"I'm afraid you'll get no more sleep today, Edibus," the king replied. "I know I won't."

The old man scowled. "Oh, wonderful. What is it?" He opened the door a little more as he studied the rest of the group. "And why have you brought an entire entourage to my door?

Have you come to carry me off to the gallows? You know I can't put up much of a fight."

The king sighed. "What would we condemn you of? Living far too long? Just let me get to the point."

The man folded his scrawny arms across his chest. "Fine, but speak fast. I may be strongly inclined to shut this door in a few seconds."

The king pushed me forward. "This is the phoenix."

The man's eyes grew huge behind his thick glasses. He took them off for a moment, squinting as he wiped them on his baby blue nightclothes. "The phoenix, you say?" he asked, putting the spectacles back on and looking me up and down. "Ah yes, I see it now."

"See what?" I asked.

"The radiance of a light being. And more importantly," he paused and pointed at the place where my sleeve had slipped slightly, "the scar."

Chapter Twenty-three

"A SCAR?" THE king said, brow creased. "I knew nothing about a scar. Did you withhold information from me?"

"I didn't keep anything from you," Edibus said simply. "You clearly didn't study *Rare Flora Lore* by Jon G. Debley as thoroughly as I did. There was a whole page on the scar that the immortal plant may leave."

King Torran frowned. "That book was almost seven hundred pages long and duller than a spoon."

Edibus shrugged. "But informative, even though most of it was a bunch of hogwash. It seems that he was right about the immortal plant."

I tilted my head. "That may explain that the plant could leave a scar, but how did you know that the phoenix would have one?"

Edibus looked sheepish. "Well…okay, I'll admit it… I may have held back just a *tad bit* of information."

"What?" the king shouted suddenly, fists balled at his sides. "It was my right to know *everything* about this!"

Edibus squinted his eyes and pointed a bony finger up at him. "And you would have found a letter and a journal under my bed, wrapped in parchment that said, *To King Torran,* which would explain everything I hadn't told you yet."

"And is it under your bed now?" the king asked.

Edibus shut the door until only his giant spectacles peeked out. "Well…no. I was planning on writing it when I felt like I was dying."

"You foolish old man," the king said, shaking his head.

"Never mind what would have been," Princess Cecile interrupted impatiently. "The phoenix is here now, and we need answers. Tell us what you know."

The old man sighed. "I suppose it is time." He threw me a quick glance. "Let me get dressed, and we'll meet in the library shortly."

The king drew out a sigh. "Fine, but I'm leaving a guard here to make sure that you follow through."

"Whatever," the old man grumbled and slammed the door.

The king turned to me. "See what we mean?" he muttered. He pushed his way through to the head of the group, and motioned for one of the guards to stay at the door.

"What if he had been killed?" he said as we made our way back down the stairs.

"I suppose it's a good thing that he lived so long," said Princess Cecile.

I glanced at the king, brow knitted. "If the royal family were the only ones who were supposed to know about the prophecy, how did Edibus find out?" I asked.

The king shot a troubled look back at me before he answered. "My father and mother were older when they finally had me. After years of trying to produce an heir and no luck, they decided to pass the information on to my father's most trusted advisor—Edibus. As ancient as he is now, Edibus was younger than my father, and he'd promised to pass on the information to the next person to ascend the throne. Then, coincidentally, my parents finally had me. They left all the tutoring to Edibus. After my father died when I was eleven and my mother when I was thirteen, it was up to him to pass on the majority of the information."

I nodded. "Well, if your father trusted him that much, he must not be too bad."

"I do trust him, and I still can't believe he didn't tell me everything. He's just…an irritating man."

"I suppose there are worse things he could be," Princess Cecile said. "And at least he's decided to tell us now."

Once we got back to the main floor, the library doors were only a few steps away. A woman bowed to us when we entered, but kept on shuffling through the papers on her desk. Through the shelves, a small sitting area could be seen. We sat there while we waited for Edibus to show up. It certainly seemed that he took his time.

There were about twenty awkward minutes of tired yawns and impatient sighs before the door opened up again, and he and the guard stepped through. He'd changed into loose clothing not so different from what he'd been wearing before. With him, he carried a small leather bound book that's binding was falling apart.

"Ed, what took you so long?" grumbled the king.

"It takes a lot longer to dress when you get older," grumbled Ed. "Not to mention I had to find this old thing." He raised the book.

The king reached for it, but Edibus, moving faster than it seems an old man should, snatched it out of reach. "Ah, ah, ah. It'll be useless if I don't find the page first."

The king slammed his fist against the arm of his chair. "Then just get to it, would you?"

Edibus cleared his throat and opened the old book. He flipped through the pages until he came to a certain one. "Ah. Here it is."

The king snatched for the book, and this time, Edibus let him have it.

He studied the page for mere seconds and then flipped the book over to the cover. "What is this? It's hand-written."

"It's the journal of Leon Baldwin, the last phoenix. Go ahead, read it out loud. I think the young lady has waited long enough," he said with a gesture to me.

The king opened the book back up and began to read.

"He says, 'I had another vision today… I watched as the great metal giant was hurled into the chasm, but it wasn't me that did it. Instead, on the top of that cliff, there was a small, red-headed girl, one that I've seen many times before in my visions. The last phoenix.

'The vision ended before I could see if she made it across the pit of lava, but I'm certain she did. I've seen her in the middle of a battlefield after she's gotten the scars.

'Since that vision, I've worked out why she has them. While the Creator let her have the plant, no human in this world is meant to be immortal. She must have consumed enough of the plant to make her more powerful than her mortal body could handle. Whether or not the plant will destroy her completely, I wouldn't be able to say. I can only hope that she accomplishes her destiny before it is too late.'"

The king turned the page, and then shuffled through the rest.

Edibus's started toward a chair. "That was his last entry, if you were trying to look for another."

The king looked at him. "Why did you keep this from me? What would have been the consequence?"

Edibus's knees creaked as he sat down. "You are duty driven. If I had told you, you would have been obsessed with looking for the phoenix, suspecting every small, red-headed girl only to be disappointed when it wasn't her. I wanted there to be enough mystery that you could only wait, instead of wasting your life looking for something that would only show up when it was ready."

The king looked down at the book. "I wouldn't have done that. I was patient enough when we heard that the phoenix had been found in Leviatha, the northern island no less."

"Only because I persuaded you to stay. I had to remind you that it was her destiny to come to Onwin in her own time."

"Fine," the king gritted out as he stood. "Maybe I would have spent my life searching for her, but that should have been up to me. You had no right to keep this a secret," he said as he raised the book.

Princess Cecile reached up and placed her hand on her father's arm. "Father, enough of this. What's done is done. The prophecy has been told, and I'm sure we could all use some rest."

The king took in a few deep breaths as he stood up straight and dropped his hand. "You're right, Cecile. Take Ivy to one of our guest suites. I'm sure you are both tired after your journey."

Then, he swept toward the door, but before slamming it behind him, he paused. "If you were any younger, Edibus, I'd throw you in a cell. You're lucky the phoenix came now instead of a decade ago."

Having heard our conversation, the librarian wouldn't stop staring at me curiously. Edibus pushed himself out of his chair and walked up to the woman. "I trust you can keep this conversation to yourself?"

The woman nodded as she turned back to her papers. "Of course, Master Edibus."

"Good." He turned to me and gave me a nod. "Rest up, young one. Destiny awaits."

After being taken to a room as gray and bleak as any other in this fortress, all I could do was toss and turn. I may have gotten in two hours of sleep, if you added all the minutes together. I would drift off for a while, and then my mind would wake up with a jolt and my heart would race, pounding in my ears as my eyes wandered around the sun-drenched room.

When the sun was high in the sky, I was awoken not by a thought, but by a voice. "Ivy," someone whispered. "Ivy."

The voice faded in and out, echoing slightly off the stone walls. I sat up straight in bed. "Who's there?" I asked, pulling the cover up to my chin.

A laugh reverberated throughout the room. Then, through the barred window, I saw him, glowing ghostly blue, slightly wavering with the wind. He walked through glass and metal as if it wasn't even there, and his feet didn't fully touch the ground.

"What are you doing here, Niko?" I asked, letting the cover drop and backing against the headboard. "How are you here?"

He put his hands up. "Relax. I can't hurt you in this form and you can't hurt me. All I want to do is talk."

"*How are you here?*" I enunciated, fighting the urge to scream for the guards standing just outside my chamber.

"I know you probably hope it after our last encounter, but I'm not dead. I'm simply taking advantage of Kurt's pendant."

My eyes widened. "How? I don't have the other half."

He smiled maliciously. "You may not have it anymore, but someone near you does. I've been watching you for a long time, Ivy. And now that I've altered the magic, I can speak to you."

There was only one person who had traveled with me to get to Onwin. "Princess Cecile. How does she have the pendant?"

He snorted. "People do such foolish things when they're afraid, particularly when it has to do with the supernatural. First it was your prince. I told him to go get the pendant and bring it back to the castle."

"And Princess Cecile?"

"I told the prince to give it to her, as a sort of apology for not marrying the girl he truly loves."

"You're horrible," I said in disgust.

"I'm cunning," he corrected. "Which is why I'm invaluable to King Ciaran."

"Why are you here? Why are you telling me all of this?"

"Partly to see the look on your face when you find out what I've been doing all along. Now I know everything. I saw the prophecy."

Dark tendrils of fear crept into my heart. "No," I whispered. Could that fact change the prophecy all together? Has my mission failed before it even began?

"But here's my question to you—how do you know you're on the right side? How do you know that the kings of Leviatha and Onwin don't have darkness in their hearts?"

I narrowed my eyes. "I don't doubt that they do. They're only human after all…It's just that some, like you and your king, have more darkness than others."

"I wouldn't judge a person's heart so soon," Niko said, folding his ghostly arms over his chest, his smirk changing into a frown.

"You brought that on yourself when you tried to force me into your Saints of Sorcery group."

He glowered at me. "Have it your way. But you don't want to be our enemy on the battlefield." He paused to collect himself and let the same small smirk curl on his lips. "But then again, you may not make it to the battlefield."

With that, he took the phantom stone off his neck and disappeared.

Heart pounding, I stepped off the bed. He knew where I was, and Princess Cecile had the other half of the pendant. I had to leave as soon as possible. I hurriedly opened the window and grabbed the bars, ready to rip them out of place if I had to. But then, I stopped to think.

Princess Cecile still had the pendant. I needed to make sure that it got as far away from the Black Fortress as possible before Niko reported every little secret detail back to King Ciaran.

I slipped my sandals on and rushed to the door. The guards looked at me questioningly, but didn't say anything as they matched my hurried pace toward Princess Cecile's room. Her guards looked up as I approached.

"I need to speak to the princess. It's urgent," I said.

They looked at the guards behind me, and something passed between them that allowed the guards to step out of the way. To avoid spearing my hand on one of the spikes, I opened the door without knocking.

I looked inside to see Princess Cecile still sleeping peacefully in her bed, undisturbed by glowing apparitions like I was.

I approached and shook her shoulder, startled when the harmless looking princess gripped my arm tightly and brought a knife out from under her pillow, death in her eyes. Then, she saw that it was only me and dropped my arm immediately.

"Couldn't knock," I said, gesturing back to the spiky door.

"Oh. Sorry," she said as she slipped the knife back under her pillow.

"Where did that come from?" I asked.

She raised an eyebrow. "Did you think I would live in a place like this and have no combat training? My father made sure I knew everything about fighting before I turned sixteen."

"Impressive," I said, ignoring my racing heart.

"Imagine going through all that training and placing so much importance on ferocity only to have the second form of a swan." She laid back in the bed with a tired groan and closed her eyes. "What do you want, anyway? Don't you have sleep to catch up on? Or did the plant give you the power to go forever without it?"

"I wish I could've let you sleep longer, but something urgent came up."

She leaned up on her elbow and cracked her eyes open again. "Well?"

I tilted my head. "Did Prince Matthias give you a black pendant?"

Her eyebrows lowered. "How did you know about that?"

I looked down at the bed cover to avoid her eyes. "Have you been seeing ghosts?"

She didn't answer straight away. I glanced back up to see that her face had gone white and pale. "Have you been seeing him, too? He told me I was the only one who could see him because I carry the pendant."

"Partly true," I said. "He wanted me to see him. But Cecile, Niko isn't a ghost."

A look of confusion, almost anger, passed across her face. "What else could he be?"

"He's a sorcerer. A spy," I answered.

Her face turned steely. "How do you know?"

"Because he was my trainer in the conservatory. I've seen him work magic."

Her eyes widened, and then water began to pool in the corners. She jumped up from the mattress and ran to the dresser across the room. After pulling it open, she tossed aside the things in the drawer, which was made up mostly of underclothes. She pulled out the phantom stone and held it out to me. "Take it. Take it far away."

I grabbed the gem and looked back up. "Shouldn't we tell your father?"

She bit her lip and shook her head. "No. He has enough to deal with without knowing that most of his secrets have been given away."

"Won't he find out eventually anyway?" I said.

"Maybe," she said, crossing her arms. "But at least for now, he doesn't have to know."

I took a step back. "Where should I take it?"

"I-I'm not sure."

"Should I just leave? To find the dragon?"

She shook her head. "Father wouldn't be happy about that, and frankly, neither would I. Isn't there more you want to learn?"

"Is there?" I asked, eyebrows raised.

She shrugged. "I don't know. If I were you, I would put it off as long as possible. Aren't you afraid of death?"

My scar felt prickly as I became aware of it. *Death is inevitable.* "What's there to fear?"

She leaned against her dresser. "Pain, of course."

I nodded. "I don't look forward to that. But Cecile, how much longer do you think I have?"

She looked back at the stone. "For what?"

"For death, for war? I might as well get going now before any of it hits," I said.

She pursed her lips. "I don't want to be the one responsible for the ruin of the kingdoms. If you think that it's best to leave now, then go ahead and leave. Just take that thing with you," she said, nodding at the pendant. "Throw it into a dark cave or something. Somewhere miles from here."

"How do I get out of here? There are bars on the windows and guards around every corner."

"Not a problem," she said. "I have an escape route." She walked to her window and pushed aside the curtains. "Most windows don't have this." She opened the window to expose the bars, but unlike mine, hers had a latch and hinges. A padlock was hooked through the bars to prevent people on the outside from opening it. Cecile pulled back the curtain a little more to expose a key hung on a nail that had been hammered to the wall.

"Hurry," she said as she handed me the key.

I disabled the lock and let the grate swing open. It made no sound.

"Are you sure you're not going to come back?" she asked.

"I don't think I have a choice," I answered.

She tilted her head to the side. "Don't you ever question the prophecy or the last phoenix? We don't know for sure if you'll die from the plant."

"But there's a chance. Besides, I'd rather have it behind me."

She sighed and then took me by surprise when she placed a hand on my shoulder. "Go. Defeat the dragon. Just know that there's a warrior here who will fight with you if the time comes."

I smiled. "Thank you."

She watched as I turned and transformed into the phoenix. It was a tight fit through the window grate, but soon, I was out in the open air, speeding away with the phantom stone gripped in my talon. I kept waiting for an alarm to sound, but there was no shout or roar or any indication that anyone had noticed my departure.

That's good. One less obstacle to worry about.

I headed east, toward the one place I suspected the dragon to reside.

I remembered the man that protected his small village on the coast from natives. He'd said he'd seen a shadow fall over the forest years ago. And I still remembered the time when my feet hit the sandy shore only to collapse under me as a roar sounded in my head.

The dragon was somewhere on the Isle of Ginsey. I was sure of it.

Chapter Twenty-four

ONWIN WAS A large country, and certainly a daunting one. There were guard towers and flight brigades everywhere. The fact that I intended to get to the Isle of Ginsey through Pira made the trek through Onwin even longer, but I'd rather a longer trek through Onwin, where I was a friend to the king, than having to go through Ginsey.

It took me two days to get to the wall of Pira, the country where I intended to drop off the pendant. During the journey, I could sometimes feel the pendant grow hotter. I assumed it was because Niko was trying to get through to me, so I would quicken my speed, hoping that in his spirit form, he wouldn't be able to keep up with me. It was probably a stupid concept, but nevertheless, I saw no sign of him. In the back of my mind, I knew that didn't necessarily mean he wasn't watching. He could be recording my every move and reporting my position to his king.

As the wall drew closer, it seemed that the prairie grass was growing thinner. From up above, the land beyond the wall appeared brown and desolate with not a drop of water in sight. With my enhanced eyesight, I could see that the men manning the wall were hot and sweating, some even daring to strip away some of their armor.

I knew it would be impossible to keep from being seen. In fact, I knew that they probably had already spotted me in the cloudless sky. To keep from being shot at with arrows, I knew my only option would be to climb as high in the sky as possible. I hefted myself upward, gaining altitude, never letting my eyes rest as I watched the men scrambling on the wall once they sensed my plan. I climbed and climbed until the air was deathly cold and so thin that it choked my breathing. Even with my keen eyesight, I could barely see the guards below.

Once I was sure that I had gone far enough past them, I angled myself downward into a dive, my lungs aching for a breath of fresh air.

I had no doubt that they would send a flight brigade after me, so there was no time to stop. I flew quickly, guided on by the wind at my back that was no doubt pushing the others faster as well.

After a few minutes of mindless flying, I noticed something on the surface. There was no water to be found, but down below, in the cracked earth, there were strange shaped green plants. At first glance, they looked like people in bizarre green clothing, holding their arms up in surrender, but when I flew a little lower, I could see that some were misshapen or surrounded by dry, dead bramble patches. A few even had blossoms on them.

After flying past hundreds of those peculiar plants, something peaked over the horizon, something that I at first thought was an odd shaped city. Then, as I got closer and closer, the shapes began to look more like blocks. Plateaus.

It took longer than I thought to pass over the first one, but after it dropped off, I noticed something on the lower ground. Rows of white tents, printed with the red snake of Pira, hundreds of armed people walking between them. The queen's soldiers.

Heart pounding, I hurried to gain altitude once again, keeping my eye out for anyone who noticed me and hoping that they would think me one of their own.

They didn't.

All at once, I heard shouting and from the largest tent, a flag flying high above it, a woman stepped out.

Immediately, I felt the feathers on the back of my neck stand up. I didn't get a very good look at her, but she was thin with raven-black hair whipping in the wind. Even in the heat, she wore a pelt of some kind wrapped around her otherwise sleeveless shoulders. She held a black spear in one hand, and raised it to the wind as I watched.

My flight faltered, and I had to strain to pick up speed. She was trying to ground me with magic.

I kept the memory of my parents in my mind and pushed onward. It was then that I heard a scream sound from below. With one glance backward, I saw the woman's spear coming toward me, but she had missed by a long shot. She now stood weaponless, glaring up at me as I got farther and farther away.

Heart pounding, I continued on. The sun was getting low and my mind and body were growing weary. Plateau after plateau passed before I came to a deep canyon, where the river had worn itself down almost a mile of solid rock. It was the first sign of water I'd seen since Onwin.

I swooped lower, keeping an eye out for any enemies that might be clinging to the sides of the cliffs. Birds flitted from cliff face to cliff face, but I could only hope that none of them were shifters. Grass crowded the bank, the water roaring through the ravine and pulling some of the greenery down into its swift current.

I dropped down until I was only a few feet from the water and opened my claw. The pendant slipped from my grasp. I watched as the water swept it downstream.

Just watching it go, I felt as if a weight was lifted off my shoulders. I flapped back up to the side of the cliff and landed on a ledge, digging my claws into the cracks to keep from falling into the river. Just having the moment to rest my wings felt wonderful. A little bit of my energy started to return.

Then, just when I was ready to take off again, agonizing pain ripped across my back. Taken by surprise, I lost my grip on the side of the cliff, and fell into the rushing water. The current dragged me down and tossed me against the rocks.

The last thing I remembered was pain splitting the side of my head, and then I was out.

When I woke up, there was a steady roar. I cracked open my eyes, scared at what I would find, but it was only a waterfall in the distance. I pushed myself up with my wings in the shallow pool I'd been pushed up into. The water was pink with blood, but there wasn't a scratch on me…besides the new scar that tingled on my back.

I shifted into first form and coughed water out of my lungs. Once I was able to take a steady breath, I studied my surroundings.

Gone was the constant orange of the desert, replaced instead with grays, greens, and browns of woodland. I wasn't sure where the river had taken me, but it had to be either southern Ginsey or northern Pira. I'd rather the latter than the first.

I reached around and traced the veins of scars that now lined my back, another reminder that I might not have much longer.

Before getting to my feet, I took in a few deep breaths and scanned the woods for anything suspicious, anything that scented my blood or my fear. From what I could tell, nothing hid in the shadows.

I took in a deep, rattled breath and closed my eyes, trying to regain my energy so I could continue the journey. I had no idea where I was right now, but I only hoped that I would still be able to find my way to the Isle of Ginsey. I opened my eyes and looked up at the sun which had sunken low behind the trees. That was west, which meant that the Isle of Ginsey would be somewhere behind me.

I changed into the phoenix and took off, circling back around until I was pointed away from the sun. The new development of the scar made flying uncomfortable. Each flap of my wings made the skin across my back feel too tight. I narrowed my eyes and pressed on stubbornly.

Just before the sun set, I studied my surroundings. Off to the right, I could see the greenery becoming sparser. That was the direction of the desert. To my left, the land rippled up into mountains. I didn't think I was in Ginsey yet, but if I went that direction, it wouldn't be long before I was. Kurt was probably just two days flight away, and yet, there was nothing I could do for him.

What if I join their side after I defeat the dragon? Kurt would be safe... I banished the thought. That was exactly what they wanted, and I knew that Kurt himself wouldn't want me to make that decision. I forced my mind to come back to the mission at hand. I just hoped that I was going the right direction.

I flew until I hit the coast, but I'd apparently been pointed in a slightly wrong direction. Though the days here were colder than they were in the desert, I still expected the island to be further north, so I angled my body toward the left, the tips of my wings cutting through the air as I shifted course.

The rain hadn't started to fall yet, but I expected it to soon. I almost hoped it would just to cool my stinging back. Nevertheless, it held off. For miles, I saw nothing but darkness below me, but then in the distance, I saw light filtering through a thick layer of fog. I headed in that direction, ever conscious of my exhaustion. I descended into the fog slowly, avoiding a few branches before finally landing on the sandy shore on the side of the mainland.

As soon as my talons touched the ground, I shifted into first form and walked toward the lake. My throat was parched and my scar ached for the cool water. I waded in until it was up to my waist, and then dove. Underwater, I could hear my thundering heartbeat in my ears. I listened as it slowed considerably in only a few seconds. I came back up for air after about a minute, shivering with cold.

I waded onto solid ground and focused my energy on drying off. The water steamed from my body, joining the fog around me. I laid down on the sand and looked up, breathing in a sigh. I closed my eyes and let the sounds of the forest lull me to sleep.

Chapter Twenty-five

THE NEXT DAY, I woke up to intense hunger pangs. I sat up and noticed immediately that any soreness I had felt the day before had since disappeared. *Thank goodness.*

The fog had already diminished a bit, and the sun was much higher in the sky than I had anticipated. I pushed myself to my feet.

I doubted that the woods on this side of the lake would have anything to catch and eat, as choked as they were by fog, so I shifted into the phoenix and backtracked to an area where the fog hadn't affected the growth of the forest.

It had been a long time since I'd hunted like this, but I was surprised to see how easy it was to catch my prey. I saw the grouse from far above, and despite its attempt to escape, I descended upon it and delivered a swift death in seconds.

After cooking and eating the bird, I tried to find some edible vegetation, knowing it would be best to store up as much energy as possible. Since the weather had turned colder, there was really nothing to find except for roots. After searching for an hour, judging by the sun, I found only parsnips. I'd had parsnips before, and hated them unless they were masked somehow in a soup.

Nevertheless, I flew my find back to the lake to wash them, and forced each one down one by one, my eyes watering at the sharp flavor.

The fog had diminished to a light dusting on the water, but nothing more. I closed my eyes, steeling myself to the task at hand. *As soon as I take off, as soon as I spot the dragon, I could be mere minutes from death.*

But I needed to survive. I needed to help Kurt escape from King Ciaran.

I spread my wings and began my trip around the island, looking for any camp or village other than the one Roland died in. I hoped I would never have to go there again. If I had to, I couldn't disguise myself. They already knew my human form, and even if I put mud all over my feathers, the size and shape of my phoenix form would give me away.

It wasn't until I was all the way around the island that I finally spotted something that looked promising. A cliff rose high above the water, and right in the center of the rock face, there was a large v-shaped gap, overgrown with snaking vines and shadows. It was only when I circled back and swooped closer that I saw the huge hole that had been ripped through the growth.

That may have been the moment when true, blood-chilling fear settled in. I barely knew what I was up against, but by the looks of it, it was even larger than I'd anticipated.

I pushed down the fear that threatened to choke me and flew closer. I landed on one of the vines, close to the top of the cliff, and looked down through the gap. I couldn't see anything, but with my wingbeats silent, I began to hear *whoosh, whoosh, whoosh.*

With dread, I realized what that sound meant and immediately scrambled deeper into the vines, hoping the monster hadn't seen me.

Despite the noise sounding very close, the dragon was still far away. I studied it as it drew closer and the beat of its wings grew louder. For some reason, I'd expected the monster to be dark colored, but instead of a black silhouette, there was a bright, white figure, the sun reflecting off its form.

I held my breath as it came close enough for me to see how its icy eyes were lined with dark blue and how the white, shard-like spikes on its back were tipped with the same color. I'd thought it hadn't seen me, that I'd been well hidden, but just before it was supposed to dive into the viney gap, it altered its course and slammed into the cliff beside me, holding on to the rock with the jagged, white hooks on the ends of its wings and the dark gray talons on each foot.

It peered through the vines with one giant ice-blue eye and let out an ear-splitting roar.

Panicked and tangled in vines, I let out a blast of fire, scorching the dragon's eye and the vines around me. The beast reared back in surprise, nearly tumbling down into the water.

I took that moment to dart past it.

To my dismay, the dragon managed to keep a hold on the cliff. I circled back, summoned up all my energy, and released a white-hot blast of fire when I got close enough to do damage. Before the fire hit, the dragon had pushed off of the wall, and hefted itself up into the air. The blaze managed to hit its chest, and the winged serpent bellowed out a pained cry, but didn't let its flight falter.

I dove away and readied myself for another attack. If I delivered a blow to its other eye, it would give me a definite advantage. The eye that I had already scorched was red and closed. I wagered that the dragon wasn't even able to open it, and may never be able to use it again.

I beat my wings against the air quickly, needing to gain altitude before I delivered my next blow. Once I felt like I was high enough, I angled my body down into a dive. An exhilarating feeling of power grew in my chest. I could do this. *I can defeat this dragon, I can be free from the prophecy and save Kurt.*

My fear vanished as I gathered the heat in my lungs for the next blow.

When the dragon opened up its great maw, I assumed it was getting ready to breathe fire. I dodged away and sent a blast to its other eye, but it turned its head just in time and dampered down my fire with icy breath.

I was taken completely by surprise. I'd thought that all dragons were fire beings. Not only did the ice freeze my fire into nonexistence, but it went beyond it to creep across my body, stiffening my movements. I plummeted toward the water, my eyes frozen open. It took all my strength to break my wings free of the icy bonds.

But I was too late. The dragon had already moved on to its next tactic. While I was trying to stay above the water, flapping frantically to get higher, it dove right in, soaking me completely. Then, it reared its great white head back up and wasted no time aiming yet another icy breath in my direction. This time, the ice was so thick, it was impossible to break free. I skidded down into the water, and everything started getting darker as I sunk further and my body was denied oxygen.

A few shreds of thought came to my mind while I went down into the murky depths of unconsciousness.

I can't die…

Kurt… He needs me.

Chapter Twenty-six

I'M NOT DEAD.

My body was cold and riddled with pain, but at least that meant that I wasn't dead. I lay stretched out on my back on a hard surface, my muscles aching and sore, a feeling that I hadn't felt much of since consuming the elixir of the plant.

Wherever I was, it was too dark to see anything. Just the fact that I was breathing and able to move was a relief. I did not expect to be in my human form, but I found myself absent of feathers, only wearing the red dress of my first form. I reached for my power, desperate for the warmth, but there was nothing. No pull of energy, no power running over my palms, nothing.

Frightened, I imagined the sunrise, but I didn't shift. It was as if the cold had stripped away any strength that I had. I fought to stand up and reached for the wall, feeling only powdery frost. As I felt my way around, it soon became obvious that I was trapped in a dome of ice.

Shivering, I sunk to the ground and wrapped my arms around myself. I don't know how long I sat there, eyes wide open in the dark, scared that I would starve to death in the tomblike ice prison. At some point, I curled into a ball on the ground and let my eyes close. I thought about Roland. How he'd found death on this island, just like it seemed that I would. I remembered the bright angel, no doubt the same one he'd seen before he left me. How long would it be before the angel came for me?

It was selfish of me, but I wished the angel would come soon so I could know what warmth felt like again.

Desperate, I pushed myself to my knees and let my elbows rest on the ground.

Lord, if I am to die, please...make it swift. I failed to defeat the dragon. I failed to complete my destiny. I failed to save Kurt. I paused as tears began to prick the corners of my eyes. I sniffled loudly. *Just keep him safe. Or if he is to die in that prison, don't let his suffering drag on...*

"Forgive me," I said aloud. The words were not only a plead to God, but to Kurt, Liana, Ayon, Cecile, and everyone else that would be caught up in a horrible, bloody war that might not have been had I been able to do what I was supposed to.

I let the tears run down my face, but the room was so cold that they froze on my cheeks. Knowing that there was no one here to listen to my sobs, I let them go, echoing in my ears in a prison that only made them louder.

It was only when I quieted that I was able to hear a crack. Surprised, I jerked up into a sitting position, and studied the ceiling, where it seemed that the sound had originated. That's when I noticed that I could see a dim light through a thick layer of frosted ice. A fissure was spreading through the ceiling. I scrambled into a corner when something dark hit the ice again. The fissure expanded, snaking out in different directions. It was hit again and the crack spread even more until finally, it caused the ceiling to come crashing down. I hugged the wall, escaping most of the falling blocks of ice, except one that hit me so hard on the head that my vision failed me for a moment.

I didn't have time to take in the outside world, though I knew it was still dark. A hand grabbed my arm and pulled me up effortlessly despite my protests.

"Stop struggling," said a gruff male voice. "You'll only hurt yourself."

I let my eyes adjust to the light, which turned out to be a lantern. The man set a fast pace as he dragged me along. I was barely able to keep up, nearly falling over rocks that appeared in our path. Still, I was thankful for the warmth. We ended up going through tunnels that I never would have been able to navigate without a source of light.

As we walked, I studied what I could see of the man in front of me. He had black, glossy hair that hung down past his shoulders, and when he turned his head to look back at me, I could see the shadow of stubble along his jaw.

"Where are you taking me?" I asked.

"Where do you think?" he said. "To the man you tried to kill yesterday."

I swallowed the lump in my throat and narrowed my eyes. "The dragon."

Maybe there was still hope after all. Maybe if I just summoned my power. I reached for it again, but even though I was out of the ice prison, my strength had not returned.

"Why can't I feel anything?" I asked, trying not to let the panic seep through into my voice.

"Feel anything?" the man asked. He shook his head. "Ask the dragon."

I kept quiet for the rest of the trek through the tunnels. When there was a light at the end of the last one, my heart sank. I would face the dragon now, and what could I do? I couldn't kill him without my power, especially if he still had his own. I was hopeless.

Before I was brought out into the light, I could see people milling about among shelters of sticks and leaves. Up ahead, I saw the gap and the vines running from cliff to cliff. I was in the dragon's den, but the fact that there were so many people around him unsettled me. I'd expected him to be a recluse, living alone, destroying everything in his path. *I guess every monster needs fearful slaves...*

When the man and I emerged from the cave, everyone suddenly stopped what they were doing and glared in my direction. One person, a young snub-nosed girl, even spat at my feet. "Filthy rat," she commented.

I blushed in anger. We were about to ascend a set of stairs carved into the side of the cliff when I thought I heard someone say my name. I looked for the culprit, scanning everyone until I saw her. Her brown hair was cut short, far different from the long hair she used to have. Roselle knitted her eyebrows in concern, looking around at the others that all seemed like they could kill me without regret. All my anger seeped away. Roselle was here and safe and *alive*.

I tripped over the first step and would've fallen on my face had the man not caught me. "For goodness sake, girl. Pay attention to your feet," he growled.

I swallowed my anger, and started up the steps, my legs feeling like lead. A domed building, made completely of ice, was frozen to the side of the cliff. I hated to go back into another ice prison, but I knew with the man dragging me that I would have no choice. We ducked into the igloo and before I could look up to see the dragon, I was blindfolded. I fought against it, but the man twisted my arm behind my back until I stilled.

"What will you do to me?" I asked, breaking the silence.

The voice that spoke was silky and smooth. "If it were a fair world, I would take your eye. You just about took mine." After a pause, he said, "Tell me, why did you attack?"

I pursed my lips, and refused to answer. If I told him that it was my destiny, he would either laugh or kill me on the spot.

"Do you work for King Ciaran?" he asked.

I gave a shake of my head, my lip curling in disgust. "Of course not," I snarled.

"Do you work for Queen Valerie?"

"No."

There was a moment of silence. Then, he sighed and ripped the blindfold off my head, allowing me to see him for the first time.

One thing was for sure. His voice certainly didn't match his face. Like his comrade, he had long hair. It was blond and curly with a beard almost as long to match. His left eye was sealed shut, a burn mark still seared on the side of it, but the open eye studied me curiously, as ice blue as I remembered.

While battling the dragon, I hadn't thought about how much it would hurt, but looking at another person, I almost felt sorry for what I did.

He lowered his eyebrows as I studied him. "You're surprisingly young. But you're powerful. I don't know who you're working for, but I can tell you this. You're on the wrong side. We're the good guys."

I snorted. "Everyone believes they're the good guys."

"And what do you believe?" asked the man with the long black hair. "Do you believe in death and destruction? Cause we're trying to stop a bloody war."

The glower vanished from my face. "How? The kingdoms are pitted against one another. There is no way out but war."

"I have a plan," said the dragon. "A plan that involves the death of two people, and no more."

"King Ciaran and Queen Valerie?" I asked.

"Precisely," he said.

I thought about it. "It'll never work," I ended up saying.

He narrowed his eyes. "Explain."

"Because to get to them, you must kill. Not only that, but people, loved ones, are disappearing, and I can't help but think that the war won't stop with just the death of the leaders. Then there will be a fight for the empty thrones and an unease against neighboring kingdoms that might still blossom into a war. If there is no leader, the people will make one."

He raised an eyebrow. "What would you do?"

I wanted to come up with a smart answer. Something that would fix everything. But the fact was... "I don't know."

"Then my plan it is." He took a step closer. I backed away and glared at him, still untrusting. "Now, I'll ask one more time. Who is it that you're working for?"

"Myself," I spat.

He looked up at his friend, and shook his head. "Okay, Erik, take her back down if you would. I'll be along shortly to reseal the dome."

I didn't want to go back there. Panicked, I said, "Wait!"

He looked down at me, eyebrows raised expectantly. "Yes?"

"I...I know someone here," I said.

He and Erik exchanged a look. "And who is that?"

"Roselle," I answered. "We went to the same school."

Erik's lip curled. "You know Roselle?"

"That's what I just said," I replied.

"Change of plan," the dragon said. "Go get her, Erik. We need to have a talk."

A few minutes later, Roselle entered the igloo, her face pale. "August," she said, with a respectful nod of her head.

August paced closer to her and looked back at me. "This girl tells me she knows you."

Roselle looked at me and bit her lip. "Yes...we used to be friends."

Erik spoke up. "Is this the girl that caused you to get sent on the quest?"

She looked up at him and nodded. "And...I know that her actions were influenced. I know the headmaster must have put this in her head."

"He didn't, though," I said. "I came on my own. I don't belong to the conservatory anymore."

She looked at me pleadingly. "Ivy," she whispered with a shake of her head. She was just trying to help me out by saying that it wasn't my fault, and in part, it wasn't. It was the fault of the last phoenix, who wrote the prophecy. A prophecy I still believed in.

I turned my attention away from her and focused back on August. "You can put me in your prison. You can lock me away in a cage of dark and cold, but I will never change my mind. And I *will* fulfill my duty."

"To kill me?" he asked. "Because then your efforts are futile."

"We'll see," I said.

He raised an eyebrow. "Yes. You will."

He motioned for Erik to bring me as he ducked out of the room. "Follow me." He descended down the stairs, moving with lithe grace. The people parted for him as he walked past the tunnel opening and around the corner. When I saw what was hidden behind the stone, my breath was taken away. It was a temple made completely out of ice, and in the center, raised on a pedestal, was an orb that held familiar golden flowers.

"The plant of eternal life," I whispered as we walked up the steps.

August turned back to me. "But not all of the plant."

He was right. The stem was cut short.

August waited for Erik, Roselle, and me to come to a stop around the plant before he touched the glass. Almost instantly, a bright light shone on his face, and the burn mark I'd left disappeared. He blinked both eyes open and met mine. "Your efforts are futile because you *can't* kill me."

And that's when I knew that I was mistaken all along, that something was horribly wrong with the prophecy.

Because to get the plant, to come out alive, the heart had to be tested. The heart had to be pure.

Chapter Twenty-seven

AUGUST DROPPED HIS hand from the orb, studying my expression. "You seem to know what this means?"

"Your heart was…" I paused and narrowed my eyes, not ready to give up everything just yet. "You consumed the plant."

"Most of it," he said. "I was told to put the rest in the orb. I hadn't known then how it would affect the area around me."

I crossed my arms, somewhat jealous that he'd been given something more than I'd gotten; knowledge. "And how is that?"

"It gives me an advantage over people, as long as I'm within range. It gives me power over who can shift."

I studied him, eyebrow raised. "Then why didn't you just take my power when I was attacking you?"

"That's the strange thing," he said, knitting his eyebrows. "I tried. Somehow, you resisted me."

I looked over at Roselle. Her eyes were wide and her mouth was closed tight, something I never knew her to be good at when we were at the conservatory.

August stepped past us, the heels of his boots clicking as he descended the stairs. "Erik, I'll meet you in the tunnels."

Erik took a hold of my arm, but before he could drag me back down to the cave, I lunged forward for the orb. Even if August had a pure heart when he got the plant, I knew that hearts could change, especially hearts that are given power. Just before I touched it, the plant was grabbed out of the way by August, who had moved abnormally quickly to get it.

"Don't," he said, eyes flaming with anger. "If you touch this, you'll die."

"Will you kill me?" I asked, flinching at how hard Erik gripped my arm.

August took in a deep breath. "Anyone who touches the orb will die unless their heart is pure."

His words pitted my own thoughts against myself. I had just said that hearts could change. Who's to say that mine hasn't?

"Maybe we should let her touch it," muttered Erik. "I won't have to keep running through the tunnels to get her either way."

Roselle slapped his arm. "Erik! Even after everything she's done, she doesn't deserve to die."

I studied Roselle. She must have lived with these people for more than half a year and she'd only known me for a week. I didn't like it, but it made sense for her to question me.

August set the orb back down on the pedestal. "Touch it if you want, but you do it at your own risk."

I studied the orb, but didn't move a muscle. Then, I looked up into his blue eyes. "I've gone through the test before. I consumed the plant, too. That's probably why you couldn't take away my shifting ability."

August, Erik, and Roselle were struck speechless. "You went through the trials?" August asked. "How long ago was this?"

"Less than a month ago," I answered. "I was sent on a quest to get the plant and bring it back to the headmaster. Roland and Kurt came with me," I looked at Roselle. "Kurt— my brother—was captured by King Ciaran, and the natives killed Roland. On my way back to King Ciaran's castle, I landed clumsily and the stem of the plant was punctured."

Roselle shook her head in disbelief. "I can't believe all that's happened to you since the last time we saw each other. Kurt is your brother?"

I nodded. "And he's still in the hands of King Ciaran."

August put his hand on Erik's shoulder. "Let her go, Erik."

Erik released me, and I stumbled away from them, unable to keep a sour expression from my face.

"Now that you know who I am, what I'm capable of, do you still think you need to attack me?" August asked.

I waited a moment before answering, "I'm not sure."

"We're going to keep you separate from the others, for your safety, but you won't need to go back to the cage," August said.

"Then where will I stay?" I asked.

"We'll make a shelter for you, but you'll have guards at all times," he said.

"For keeping me in or keeping them out?" I asked.

He raised an eyebrow. "What do you think? You tried to kill me, and even though I heal quickly, I'm not too fond of pain."

He began to lead the way back toward the main area. "How long will you keep me here?" I asked bitterly.

"Until King Ciaran is dead," he answered.

I clenched my jaw.

Erik pushed me forward. "Just because you told your sob story doesn't get you off the hook. You're still accountable for your actions."

Roselle narrowed her eyes at him. "Even so...Shouldn't we do something about her brother?"

He shrugged. "That's up to August. But in my opinion, we can't afford to try. If we alert Ginsey that we exist, all our plans will be ruined."

As we rounded the corner, I hoped that I'd be able to stay in a shelter or tent, and not some igloo. If anything, ice would only weaken me further.

From behind me, Erik spoke up. "Roselle, go see if Aryl can gather people together to find supplies for another hut."

Without questioning him, Roselle hurried away to complete the task. The people didn't crowd me as much on my way back through them, but I still received threatening glares and angry mutters.

When we reached the farthest possible point in the gap, we found a small clearing large enough for another hut. "Looks like you're running out of room," I mused.

"Only out here," he replied. "We can expand into the tunnels if needed."

"Why haven't you?" I asked.

"August likes to keep an eye on us. To make sure we abide by his rules."

"What gives him the right to rule over all of you like this?"

He looked at me as if the question were stupid. "Have you seen his second form? He's a force to be reckoned with and a protector to all who live here."

"Have there ever been any threats besides me?" I asked.

"Well, of course," he said. "There are spies from Ginsey and Pira looking for us. They would attack if he didn't keep us safe. Plus the natives aren't the friendliest of people, as you can tell by what happened to your friend."

"The natives aren't that bad. The girl that works as their healer is from the same school as Roselle and me."

"Oh, we know some of them are not from here," he replied. "But they brainwash them to think the same way. To wear funny clothes and paint their faces and act like savages."

A snort came from behind us, and I looked back to see a woman with wispy blond hair tucked up into a hair tie. Her face was creased with shallow wrinkles, mostly frown lines. "Have you ever even seen one of the natives?" she asked. "How would you know any of that?"

"From what you and some of the others have told me."

"They may wear funny clothes and paint their faces, but they are not savages," she said. "They're unhappy that we've taken up residence on their island, but they are not unreasonable. As long as we stay on our section, they won't cause any trouble."

"Only because they know August is one of us," Erik said, still unwilling to change his way of thinking. "They know that he can freeze every one of their villages if it comes down to it."

She shook her head. "Whatever you say." Then, she turned to me and grimaced. "We're only building you a shelter to keep you in," she said through bared teeth. "Otherwise, we'd let you sleep on the rock, exposed to the cold winds."

I looked away, thinking it best not to reply. I only looked back up when I heard more footsteps coming closer. There were two women and a man bringing over wooden beams, rope, and a stack of palm fronds.

"Is this the last of it?" Aryl asked.

The man nodded as he set an armful of things down on the rock.

She rubbed her chin. "We'll have to get August to take us back out tomorrow. I don't like being out of supplies."

The man started to set up the beams, fastening them together. The women waited to the side until the frame was built, and then started weaving the rope from beam to beam, creating a net that would hold each of the large leaves in place. The little hut took less than an hour for them to make.

When they were finished, Aryl kicked my shin and pointed to the shelter. "Get inside," she said, her dark eyes narrowed.

"And be thankful. August could have just let you die in the ice dome. I know I would have."

I dug my nails into the skin of my palm, trying to calm myself. I had already caused enough trouble without having another riot right here where people could see.

I ducked my head and crawled into the small shelter. There was no pillow or anything to rest my head on. The rock was hard and bumpy, but I was still glad to be somewhere other than the ice cage. Aryl let me get situated before she slammed the door.

"Don't get any ideas," Erik said to me from outside. "You're powerless here."

I hugged my knees to my chest and rested against the wooden frame. It moved backward a little. "Stop moving," he snapped.

I scoffed. "You know, I don't get the point of this," I said, peering out through the cracks. "How is this shelter supposed to keep me in?"

"You'll stay in there if you know what's good for you," he said.

I stayed quiet for a moment, and then adjusted into a cross-legged position. "And what do I do if I have to...relieve myself?"

He sighed. "Then I'll get Aryl or one of our other strong women to escort you into the caves where all the rest of us go."

"Okay," I said, an idea forming in my head. "Well, I have to."

He groaned. "Why did I get put on babysitting duty?" he muttered under his breath.

"Aryl!" he shouted. I heard the woman's footsteps, and peeked out to watch her come closer. Erik explained my predicament and Aryl griped about it just as much as he did.

Then, she opened the door. "Get out of there, girl. Let's make this fast."

I crawled back out and stood up. She reached forward to grab my arm, but before she could get a grip, I darted away, sprinting as fast as I could toward the edge of the cliff, where I heard the sound of rushing water. Behind me, there was shouting and running footsteps, but I didn't care. I leapt from the edge, only hoping that I didn't land on the rocks.

Down, down, down I fell, and just when I thought I would plunge into the water, my descent suddenly stopped.

I was floating in midair, still shaking with the adrenaline of the fall. A mix of questions flew through my head, but it only took one answer to still them.

"You shouldn't have done that," said Roselle.

Chapter Twenty-eight

"PLEASE, ROSELLE," I said, staring at the invisible point where I'd thought I'd heard the voice. "Please just let me drop."

"Pull yourself together," she whispered fiercely.

I didn't have time to say anything more since she'd already lifted me to the top, where not only Erik and Aryl stood, but just about everyone in the gap. August was pushing through them to get to me.

"What happened?" he asked, his eyes narrowed suspiciously.

"She jumped off the cliff, sir," reported Erik.

"Using her bodily functions as an excuse to make a run for it, I might add," said Aryl.

My face reddened.

He pinched the bridge of his nose and closed his eyes. "For goodness sake, woman. Why would you do that?"

"My brother," I answered.

"Your brother?"

Roselle, who had taken her visible form again, cleared her throat and spoke up. "I assume she wants to break him out of prison."

I looked back at August, and for a moment, I thought I saw understanding in his eyes, but it was quickly replaced by annoyance. "And you thought that suicide would help him somehow?"

"Believe it or not, I heal quickly when I'm out of your range," I said. "Even if I accidentally hit the rocks, I would've been fine moments later, and then I would be able to leave."

"You would only be fine if I let you be fine. The river below is in my range. But assuming you escaped, then what would you do?" he asked.

I shrugged. I didn't really know. I didn't want to hand myself over to King Ciaran so that he could work his blood magic on me, but at the same time, I didn't have a much better plan than the first time I'd tried to storm the castle on my own.

August looked around at his people. "As you were," he commanded.

He took me by the arm and pulled me out of earshot of everyone but Erik, who followed us. "If you'll stop acting unreasonably, maybe we could work out a deal."

I crossed my arms across my body. "What sort of deal?"

"If you become an asset to us, I'll help you find your brother."

The deal seemed almost as bad as what King Ciaran was offering. Joining the enemy, joining a man that the prophecy said I was supposed to defeat. However, at this point, I had no other choice. I was at his mercy.

With a nod of my head, I replied, "Fine. Deal."

He pointed to the shelter that had been made for me. "Then go where you're supposed to."

Reluctantly, I did as he said, and got in the shelter before shutting the door behind me without having an escort. "Watch her, Roselle," I heard him say. "And Erik you stay with them. This shouldn't be hard."

I folded my arm under my head and listened to the chatter of the people outside. The voices sounded angry at first, but as time passed, they got less so. Soon, I began to hear laughter, the lighthearted shouts of children, and their parents calling after them when it came time to eat. Just the smell of whatever they'd cooked made my stomach rumble. I tried to ignore the feeling of hunger. When I had my power, hunger rarely plagued me, but being without it, I was a whole lot more vulnerable than before.

I closed my eyes and tried to sleep, hoping it would ward off the uncomfortable feeling, and it did.

But then I woke up with the same pain and a parched throat. Darkness had crept up on me while I slept, but I still could smell food. I felt around the rock floor of the shelter, but there was nothing. No food, no water. I stayed awake for a while, listening to the sound of people winding down for the night. I figured I would chance peeking out of the shelter to see who I could ask to escort me to the caves. Through the leaves, I thought I saw Aryl and some other woman sitting with their backs against the stone wall, whispering among themselves so quietly even I couldn't hear it.

"Hello?" I said.

Aryl stopped in midsentence and turned to me. She pushed herself to her feet, eyes glinting. "Well, now, look who finally woke up. What is it?"

"I need to go to the caves."

She leaned down closer to the cage and lowered her voice. "If it were up to me, you would live with yourself and your filth in there. I'm only letting you out because I know that August would disapprove."

I heard a lock click the door opened. I tried to crawl out, but she pushed my head back inside forcefully.

"Ah, ah, ah. Hands first," she snarled.

I didn't want to make the wait any longer, so I stuck my hands out while she roped them together tightly, pinching my wrists. She kept a tail of the rope for herself and dragged me out, keeping up a fast pace even though my muscles were still getting used to walking after being cooped up in the shelter for so long.

On my way to the tunnel entrance, I saw August from afar, talking and laughing with an older woman. Everything that he seemed to be went against everything I thought I was going to do. I was supposed to destroy this man who seemed so kind and perfect, whose own plans aligned with my own more or less? It just didn't seem right.

While I watched, he glanced at me and the smile left his face. He said something else to the old woman and turned away, heading back up the stairs to his igloo, all the while with a dark expression cast upon his features.

I spent five days in that cramped shelter, receiving only one meal and a pitcher of water a day. If I needed to go to the caves, my hands were always roped first and I had an escort. The only way to pass the time was to watch the village through the cracks. Sometimes I would see August out there, talking to people, helping with various tasks. Other times I would only see his dragon form flying to and from what I suspected to be hunts, most of the time with people on his back.

He never talked to me again, which made me angry. We had made a deal that if I cooperated, he would help me rescue Kurt. I wondered if he was waiting for me to break so he could go back on his deal.

After five days, I was beginning to grow restless. Why were we wasting time? If we didn't act now, the war would start. And if he didn't let me out soon, I would attempt to escape again. I could already tell that Aryl and Erik and the other guards were getting more careless each time I went to the caves. I decided on the fourth day that I'd had enough, that I'd try to escape the next day after they brought me my meal.

Then the fifth day came. I waited in the shelter, expecting my meal at noon, but as I watched out the crack, the cook never came with the tray. I was beginning to worry that they had forgotten to prepare me something and I'd have to leave on an empty stomach. After a few more hours with nothing, I suddenly saw August emerge from his staircase. To my surprise, instead of conversing with his people, he made his way straight toward me.

I straightened my dress, wide eyes staring through the cracks in anticipation. August motioned for the guard to open the door and let me out. I was embarrassed that I was covered in filth and probably smelled terrible, but I didn't know why it mattered. He was the one keeping me this way.

Once I was out and had dusted myself off, he said, "I bet you're wondering when we are going to leave for the castle."

I nodded wordlessly.

"We've decided to go next week, as long as preparations are put in order on time and everything goes well," he said.

In other words, he was telling me to behave myself.

"Since you've stayed in that shelter for five days without fighting, I've decided to give you a little freedom. You'll be staying in Roselle's tent. She volunteered to keep you."

I smiled, relieved. "And will I still have guards with me everywhere I go?"

"Do you want help rescuing your brother?" he said.

I nodded hesitantly.

"Then no, you won't have guards. But if you do something irresponsible or destructive, I'll be forced to put them back in place, and I fear that your brother might stay in prison until everything is over."

I narrowed my eyes. "Then you can trust that I will be on my best behavior."

"I believe you," he said, and then he turned and walked away.

Aryl followed after him, and I was left alone, facing a whole community of people that probably would've rather seen me hung up in the stocks.

I walked through the crowd, feeling small and defenseless more than I felt free. Instead of the hostile glares five days before, the people either ignored me or frowned as I walked past. After such an uproar on the first day, I was surprised that no one acted out against me. Maybe as I watched August walking around and talking to everyone, he'd mentioned the plans concerning me. Among the shelters, few of them were tents. I was lucky that Roselle's was the first one I came across.

Unlike the other people, who dressed warmly, she'd shed her coat and rolled up her sleeves as she stacked wood from a makeshift wheelbarrow against the wall beside her tent.

"Shouldn't the men do all the heavy-lifting?" I asked.

She looked up at the sound of my voice. "He finally let you out, huh?"

I nodded, looking down at my dirt-covered dress.

She went back to stacking. "As for the wood, it's up to everyone to do their own share in the gap. The men are the ones that go out and get it, with August's help, of course."

"Sounds like all of you depend on August too much." I paused. "What if he died out there? You would all be stuck."

She raised an eyebrow. "I'm the backup. If I see anyone fall, I catch them. If anyone has permission to get out, but August is busy, I take them up to the top of the cliff."

I felt stupid for not thinking of that before. "Right." I paused. "August said I'll be staying with you."

"I know," she said with her back turned. "Despite all that's happened, I still count us as friends. But there's one condition." She hefted the last log onto the pile and turned to me.

"A condition for our friendship?" I asked.

She set her mouth into a firm line. "You have to stop finding ways to hate August. I don't know what you've been told, but he's not a bad person. He's a good leader...a kind leader. All of us would follow him into battle if he gave the word."

She watched me, waiting for an answer.

It was an inward struggle, but eventually I said, "August and I worked out a deal, and I intend to keep my end of it... But I don't know if I can ever trust him."

She gave a nod. "That'll work." She shrugged her coat back on and pulled aside the fabric of the tent. "Welcome home."

Chapter Twenty-nine

I WOKE UP to hushed whispers outside the tent, even though the sun had not yet risen. I turned my head, and my eyesight focused enough to see that Roselle was not in her bed. Of course not. I recognized her voice outside, along with a deeper, masculine voice that also sounded somewhat familiar. He was talking so softly that I couldn't exactly place it.

"...that isn't right. You should have told me from the start," said Roselle.

"I didn't know——"

Roselle cut the man off. "Didn't know what? You were leading me on, for heaven's sake! I was the one in the dark!"

"Roselle, calm down. You'll wake up the girl," he said pleadingly.

There was a moment to silence, and then I heard a sniffle. "This isn't fair. We'd made plans."

"I know," he said. "And you can't imagine how much I wish we could go through with them."

Another pause. "You shouldn't have let it…shouldn't have let us…get this far," she finally said. "I'd thought…well, never mind what I'd thought."

"I'm sorry," he said. "I didn't know that she…"

"I don't want to hear your apology, Erik," Roselle snapped, and then whipped the tent flap aside.

I closed my eyes quickly and evened out my breathing, hoping she didn't notice that I was awake. She settled down on her mat, and for a moment, all was quiet…until she took in a shuddering breath. I wasn't sure what to do, so I just laid there, listening to her sob quietly.

After less than a minute, I couldn't take it anymore. "Roselle?"

Her sobs quieted.

I let a few seconds pass before asking, "What's wrong?"

She sighed shakily and rested her head back on the mat. "I might tell you in the morning… We both need our sleep right now."

"If there's anything I can do—"

"Don't worry about it, Ivy," she barked.

I went quiet, but I had my own suspicions. It sounded as if Roselle had been involved in a relationship with Erik and some woman stood in the way.

I settled back down and gazed up at the tent canvas until I finally fell into a restless sleep.

The next morning, I awoke to find Roselle missing. I threw aside the covers and padded outside, squinting as I looked around the gap. A cart of firewood rattled across the stone in front of me, pushed by an old woman I had seen August talking to a couple times before.

"About time you got up," she grumbled. "Why don't you help me with this wood?"

Without complaint, I took the handles from her, deciding that talking to Roselle would have to wait until later. The woman led the way at a snail's pace. We ended up making three trips back and forth from the firewood pile and by the end, my hands were covered in splinters and I'd bruised my foot when I accidentally dropped one of the heavier logs. Without my healing power, small things like that were starting to bother me.

After leaving the old woman, it wasn't long before others started to ask for my help. I swept and tidied several shelters, assisted a man whose shelter needed repairing, and dug up potatoes from the garden, and still, there was no sign of Roselle.

At lunchtime, I sat with my earnings of the morning—a bowl of thin vegetable stew—when she suddenly appeared in front of me. I flinched and soup sloshed over the edge of the bowl onto my dress.

"Roselle!" I said as I tried to wipe the soup out of the fabric. It wasn't as if I could change into something else now that August controlled my shifting ability.

She managed a small smile. "Sorry. It's a habit of mine."

I set the bowl aside. "To scare the wits out of people?"

She sat up against the wall next to me. "Of course."

"Where have you been all day?"

She pulled her knees up to her chest. "Flying over the island. I just felt like I needed to get away for a while."

"What happened last night?"

Her brown eyes flickered into something darker. "Erik and I...we were planning on getting married. He'd had a wife before. I knew that. But he'd thought she was dead." Her eyes glistened with tears, and she blinked them away rapidly. "Then, last night, she showed up here."

My heart ached for her. "How did she find this place?"

"August found her. She said she was running away from Ginsey, so he took her in."

Roselle's gaze flicked to the side. "Look," she said, nodding behind me.

As if on cue, I saw Erik coming out of a shelter, the woman trailing behind him. Her dark hair was tangled up into a single, unruly knot on her head. She glanced around the gap with wild eyes before trailing behind her husband to sit at their fire. He spooned something out of their cast iron skillet into a bowl, handed it to her, and then looked up in our direction.

His eyes fixed on Roselle, and with a look of pain, he moved his chair away from her and toward his wife.

I looked back at Roselle. Her face was crumpled in the expression of someone with a broken heart. "I'd thought I was ready to face it again. But I'm just not." And with that, she vanished. A gust of wind blew my hair back, and I could only assume that that meant she was gone.

I sighed and picked my bowl back up, downing the rest of the soup in a single gulp. I stood and took the bowl back to the shelter of the woman who had given it to me, and when I turned, I recoiled.

August stood right behind me, arms crossed, his long hair pulled up into a short ponytail. He raised an eyebrow at my reaction. "Are you ready for a hunt?"

"A hunt?" I pointed to the sky. "Out there?"

He shook his head. "In the woods, not the sky. You'll still be in first form."

I frowned, disappointed. I was ready to be rid of all the little bruises and cuts that plagued my body. "How will I get out there?"

The corners of his mouth pulled up. "The same way all the others do. By climbing on my back."

I hesitated. Climb onto the back of the dragon and trust that he wouldn't drop me to my death? Or stay here, safe and sound, running errands?

August tilted his head toward the boulder where I'd seen others climb on his back before. "Up for the challenge?"

I set my jaw. "Fine."

He swept his hand in front of him. "Lead the way."

I forced one foot in front of the other. "What about weapons? You trust me with them?"

"If you were going to hurt one of us, you'd have found a way to do it."

I huffed out a breath and began climbing the wooden steps attached to the side of the boulder. When I circled around to the top, August had already shifted into his dragon form, his leathery, white wing hooked to the rock. He craned his neck back and looked at me expectantly.

I hesitated and looked out at the gap. People had begun to watch. I glanced at August, and his dragon eyes seemed to crinkle in amusement.

I pursed my lips and stepped out onto his wing, surprised at how easy it was to cross. Though his wing looked like it was made of ice, the surface was actually rough and easy to climb over. Getting onto his back was the tricky part. I had to avoid spearing myself on the shard-like spikes that lined either side of his spine. The only place I could settle was the spot where his neck met his back. There were no spikes except for the one I held on to, which fortunately, was more rounded off than the others.

Before I could even shout that I was ready, August climbed up onto the rock and launched himself into the air. I held on for dear life as we gained altitude, and then, he swooped out of the gap and into the light of the sun.

Chapter Thirty

My FEAR MELTED away, and the sun greeted me like an old friend. As we circled around to the top of the cliff, I let go of the spike with a sigh and stretched my arms out, letting the wind whisper through my fingers.

I missed flying, missed having my wings spread out like August's, capable of going anywhere.

I was forced to bring my arms back in and hold on tight to August when he landed heavily on the top of the cliff. He tilted to the side, and outstretched his wing for me to climb down.

I picked my way to the ground, trying to be even more careful since the descent was steeper than the ascent.

Once my feet were planted firmly on the rock, August shifted into his human form.

"You did pretty well for your first time," he remarked, his eyebrows lifted. "Usually, people scream or yelp when taking off and landing, but you didn't make a sound."

I shrugged. "You probably don't have many people with the second form of a bird getting on your back."

He gave a nod. "Maybe." He started into the woods, waving for me to follow.

The wind whistled through the trees as we entered the thick undergrowth of the forest. We didn't go far before August stopped at a tree with a trunk as big around as a dragon's foreleg—I would know.

Its dead branches twisted up into the sky, and its roots plowed into the earth, creating a hollow at the base. August knelt and reached inside, pulling out two bows and a quiver of arrows.

He kept the quiver for himself, but handed me one of the bows and a single arrow. "I'll give you one shot, but if something goes amiss, I'll need to be able to fix it."

"You doubt my shooting ability?" I asked.

"I didn't say that. But I know you're not used to the bow."

I studied it. The bow was a bit smaller and the curve sharper than what I was used to.

I was surprised at how silently August could move, even as we descended steep hills and walked across beds of dead leaves. Every once in a while, when I would accidentally step on a twig, his body would tense, but he didn't turn back to correct me.

Finally, after what seemed like an hour of walking in silence, we spotted a buck. His antlers rose into eight beautiful points, his body strong and thick from the plentiful vegetation.

August looked back to tell me to aim, but I already had the bow loaded and drawn back. The buck was facing us, but as soon as he turned to the side…

I was caught off guard when August tilted my aim slightly to the left and drew my arm back further. My muscles trembled with the effort to keep the weapon steady.

When the buck turned, August stepped back and said, "Shoot."

I let loose the arrow and it embedded into the deer's heart with a thud, killing it instantly.

He nodded his approval as he jumped down into the gulley. "Good job. This will help feed us for a week."

"I would've missed," I said as I followed him.

"Those are long bows we traded for with the natives. You did pretty well, having never shot one before," he explained.

He hefted the deer up onto his shoulder as if it was nothing. I'd forgotten that the plant made him strong, as it once had done for me.

"We're done?" I asked.

He nodded. "For today. We got lucky."

As we trekked back, August didn't worry about being quiet anymore. "So…your brother. What's he like?"

"A little intimidating. I know I was a bit frightened when I first met him."

He looked over, brow creased as we started up another hill. "What do you mean when you first met him?"

I breathed hard as we climbed, feeling out of shape. "I grew up in an orphanage. Didn't know I had family left until it dawned on me that Kurt looked a lot like my mother, from what I remembered of her."

"And he cares about you?" August asked.

"Of course. They're torturing him just because he won't tell them anything about me."

"How do you know that?"

I explained the phantom stone to him. How it allowed me to visit Kurt in prison without anyone knowing. Until Niko found it, anyway.

He listened, darkness cast upon his features. "We'll get him out, Ivy," he finally said. "Stick with us and we'll get him out."

I hoped he was right. I couldn't imagine that anyone would be able to beat an immortal dragon. Except, perhaps, an army of sorcerers.

"What about you?" I asked suddenly. "What of your family?"

He scowled and looked away. "The gap people are my family."

"Did you have a mother and father, though?" I asked.

He was quiet for a long time. Then, "My mother is dead. My father may as well be."

I was surprised. It didn't sound like his story was much different from my own. "My father works for King Ciaran," I said quietly. "He's my brother's torturer."

August narrowed his eyes. "I'm sorry to hear that."

We finally reached the knotted old tree, and August placed our bows under it, pulling out a bundle of rope instead.

I eyed the rope. "Are we going to be tying the deer to your back?"

He shook his head. "We'll be lowering it down into the gap."

I sighed in relief. The last thing I wanted do was navigate the spikes on August's back while dragging a deer up after me.

When we reached the cliff, he began to ravel the rope around one of the boulders, knotting it tightly after it was wrapped around three times. Then, he tied the other end around the deer's haunches and lowered it over the cliff on his hands and knees.

I sat back and watched as he lowered the buck down slowly, muscles rippling in his arms.

A holler sounded from below and he paused, waiting until a second shout rang out. Then, he gathered the rope in loops around his arm, untied it from the boulder, and said, "I'll be right back," as he ran into the woods, no doubt to store it back under the tree.

I walked to the very peak of the cliff while he was gone, looking out at the lake.

The prophecy was wrong. There wasn't an evil bone in August's body. He was kind and hard-working. He didn't expect anything of his people that he wouldn't do himself.

That night, the people celebrated over our catch. It was amazing how the ones that glared at me in hatred were now patting me on the back and congratulating me even though it was really August's kill.

Even Roselle managed a smile. "You're starting to become one of us," she said.

I smiled. "It's not so bad here."

"And August?" she asked.

I glanced away, suddenly shy. "He's not so bad either."

When I looked back, she was looking at me out of the corner of her eye, her eyebrows raised.

"What?" I asked.

"Oh, nothing," she said as she started through the shelters. "I'm off to bed."

"Goodnight," I called after her.

I finished my meal and stood to return my bowl to the cook. When the plump woman took my bowl, she gave me a nod and a smile. Then, she looked behind me and the smile faltered.

I turned to meet a wide-eyed stare, partly hidden by frazzled black hair.

Erik's wife.

"You're the phoenix, aren't you? The one who attacked the dragon?"

I frowned. I didn't like that the topic had come up, but I nodded. "Yes, that's me."

She nodded back fervently. "Okay." She studied me a little longer, and then with a small smile, she backed up and walked away.

I squinted after her, confused. Erik's wife certainly had…issues, to say the least.

As I headed back to the tent, my eyes caught August's, who still sat at the campfire, surrounded by people.

He gave a nod, and I returned the gesture.

When I entered the tent, Roselle's eyes were already closed and she was breathing deeply. I took off my sandals and settled down on my mat across from her, closing my eyes until all the thoughts came to a stop.

Voices outside quieted as more and more people followed our example.

Just as I was about to sink into slumber, I heard a clatter and a scream, and then the shouted words, "We're under attack!"

Chapter Thirty-one

Roselle and I bolted upright just as we heard more screams sounding all around us.

I hurried to the tent entrance and peeked out into the darkness. The firelight danced across the shelters, and the only thing I could see of the enemy was their flashing blades.

I ran out of the tent, shoeless on the rough rock. Then, I saw one of them.

He wore black to match the night, but I could clearly see the Ginsian insignia on his uniform. His eyes glinted as he walked from shelter to shelter, setting each one ablaze with the torch in his hand, driving the gap people out of their homes.

Nearby, I watched as a little boy was dragged out of a shelter by the scruff, his mother screaming, trying to break the man's hold.

A *whoosh* of wind blew my hair forward, and Roselle appeared beside them. She took hold of the man's shoulders, jerking him back as she shifted into the wind spirit again. The man flew above the flames, limbs flailing, and plummeted into the gorge.

I ran after the man with the torch, weaponless, hoping my training in hand to hand combat would pay off somehow. I'd anticipated taking him by surprise, but the arsonist turned just as I approached, a sneer cast upon his features.

Fortunately for me, a shadow dashed up from behind him, tackling the man to the ground. The torch went rolling, but not before I saw the long black hair and stubbly chin of Erik as he set to beating the man's face with his fist. A sickening crunch sounded, and whether it was Erik's knuckles or the man's nose, I couldn't say. Probably both.

Only once the man was rendered unconscious did Erik unsheathe the Ginsian sword and toss it to me. I caught it by the hilt.

He wiped blood from his face with the back of his hand. "You should know to fight someone your own size when you're without a weapon. But thanks for being on our side."

I raised the sword in response. "Thank you."

He glanced away as another scream penetrated the air. "Protect as many people as you can," he ordered, and then he darted off.

I stepped over the unconscious man and hurried between the shelters, eyes searching for an enemy. Above me, another invader flew through the air, bellowing. Roselle was certainly doing her part.

A woman and her daughter scurried past me, toward the caves. I was about to make sure they got there safely when I heard a shuffle in the shadows. I turned just as a woman stepped into the light, blood and dirt smudged across her sharp features. The Ginsian insignia she wore was spattered with dark red droplets, and by the way she held two stained blades in each hand, I knew she was a force to be reckoned with.

Her dark eyes glimmered. "I think I've seen you before."

"You may have," I said, crouching defensively with my blade held out in front of me.

She circled me. "My king wants you on our side. You don't have to fight. You can just sit back and watch."

I gritted my teeth. "I don't believe in slaughtering innocent people."

One corner of her mouth rose higher than the other. "I was hoping you'd say something like that."

She lunged forward, crossing her blades in a deadly maneuver that could've taken my head off. The metal rang as I deflected the blow, sending tremors through my arm with the force. She backed off as she calculated her next move, twisting the blades in her hands.

She struck again, swiping both swords at the same time. I jumped back, but one tip caught my side, cutting deep into the flesh.

I gasped through the pain as I deflected the next strike and the next. With every blow, I was getting weaker.

A triumphant gleam shone in her eyes. She could tell.

Desperate, I gathered all my energy and lunged forward right after her swords sliced through the air in front of my throat.

Her smile wavered as my sword struck home. She looked down at the blade still stuck in her chest and fell to her knees. I drew it out quickly in case she was still strong enough to land another blow.

One of her swords clattered to the ground as she dropped a hand to steady herself. She looked back up at me. "You've won." She paused as she gulped in a breath. "But then again…the more you kill, the more haunted your dreams will become. That's the cost of…having a conscience." She drew her lips into a smile and sunk to the ground. Her eyes blinked once, and then her face went slack, her pupils staring up blankly at the rising smoke.

I gripped my side and turned away from her, staggering toward the caves.

That's when I saw Roselle. She was standing in half form in front of a cowering figure, her skin so pale it was almost translucent, her long hair shining white around her.

Two attackers were closing in on her. She stretched her hands out and sent a gust of wind to blow them both back.

As I watched, the cowering figure she protected rose up.

Erik's wife.

Her hair still framed her face in wild tangles, but her features were cool and collected as she raised a dagger above her head.

The pain in my side forgotten, I sprinted forward, adrenaline surging as I lifted my blade. "Roselle, behind you!" I shouted.

The madwoman glanced over, distracted for a moment, and it gave me the time to send my sword flying through the air. It speared her right through her core.

She collapsed, the dagger dropping from her hand.

Roselle sunk down to the ground beside her with a cry. "Ivy, what have you done?"

I didn't get to answer. Instead, I stumbled back, stunned as I looked down. The tip of a blade protruded from my stomach.

I fell as the blade was jerked out.

"Ivy!" Roselle screamed.

The shout echoed in my mind as my eyes drifted closed. I sucked in a raspy breath and exhaled one last time.

Someone pushed me onto my back and stroked my hair away from my face. "Ivy." The voice was deep and sounded far away. "Ivy, wake up. You're going to be fine."

My heartbeat pounded in my ears, slow and still faltering.

And then, it picked back up, faster, faster, until it raced in my chest. Power flooded through my veins, sudden and burning. I opened my eyes to meet August's ice blue ones.

My wounds stung as they began to stitch themselves and my breathing regulated. I pushed myself up into a sitting position, and August clasped my arm, helping me stand.

He'd given me my power back.

I studied the burning shelters, the flame flickering high on the gap's walls. August stood back next to Roselle as I shifted into half form.

I narrowed my eyes and walked toward the fire, arms spread out as I soaked in the heat. Little by little, the blaze went out until the only light in the gap was the bright swirls on my skin. The screams stopped. Everything was silent.

And then, one by one, the enemy filtered out of the shelters like moths drawn to a flame.

Roselle, August, and I dove into action, an unstoppable force of wind, ice, and fire. The Ginsians didn't stand a chance.

August formed swords of ice and fought with deadly precision.

I sent blasts of flame toward anyone that tried to attack.

And Roselle chased down the ones that tried to get away, sweeping them effectively into the gorge.

Within minutes, every enemy in sight lay motionless.

Roselle appeared next to me. "I think it's over," she said, breathing hard.

And then, the man from earlier, the man that had been setting the shelters ablaze, appeared out of the gloom. His face was bloodied and one of his eyes had swelled shut. He pointed a finger at August. "He knows where you are, Prince Darren," he said with a crazed laugh. "Your father…he'll find you."

And then, there was the sound of blade entering flesh, and the man sunk to the ground, Erik holding a bloody knife behind him.

Chapter Thirty-two

AUGUST STOOD STOCK-STILL, staring at the man who had fallen.

He's King Ciaran's son?

Erik stooped down to clean the bloody blade on the man's clothes. "I'm sorry, Your Highness. I should have killed him when I had the—" He cut off his words when his eyes finally focused on his dead wife, sword still embedded in her body, blood pooling on the rock around her.

The knife he'd been cleaning clattered to the stone as he walked toward the woman he loved. He fell to his knees beside her. "No," he whispered as he stroked her face. And then louder, a cry of agony, "NO!"

Roselle stepped forward and placed a hand on his shoulder. "Erik—"

"Don't touch me," he snarled. He brushed the hair away from his wife's face and placed a kiss on her forehead.

Roselle looked beaten. Broken.

She backed away from him and glanced at me, narrowing her eyes. *You killed her. This is your fault,* they seemed to say.

Then, she turned from both of us and retreated, heading toward the caves.

My gaze flicked over to August—or Prince Darren—only to find that he'd left. It was just Erik, his dead wife, and me, the girl that killed her.

If he'd known that I'd done it, I had no doubt that he would try to end my existence.

But I'd saved his other love's life. His wife would've stabbed and killed her, and she probably led in the Ginsian attack, too. He just didn't know that yet.

I shifted into first form and backed away into the darkness. From the direction of the caves, flickering lights were emerging, all headed this way. Soon, they would happen upon Erik and his wife, and if any of them had witnessed me kill her, I didn't want to be found anywhere near him.

I turned away, unsure of what to do, where to go. I picked my way through the charred remains of shelters and ended up climbing the steps of the ice temple, where August kept the plant of eternal life.

I stopped on the last step when August's voice rang out behind me. "What are you doing here?"

I wasn't exactly sure. I turned back to him. "I—I was just worried that—"

"That someone had stolen the plant?"

I didn't reply.

He walked up the steps and brushed past me. He crouched by the foot of the pillar that the plant rested on, and gestured to the ground. "Look closely."

I shifted into half form as I approached. I studied him nervously. *How can I trust someone related to King Ciaran?*

Regardless of the uneasiness that knotted in my stomach, I came up beside him. The light from my skin illuminated something I hadn't noticed before. Ash. Black, powdery ash.

My thoughts were brought back to the final trial to get to the plant, how the angels would barely touch the demons with the tips of their swords before they disintegrated into black dust.

"So someone did try to get to it," I concluded.

August nodded. "The plant can protect itself."

I stood and looked at the perfectly preserved golden flowers. It was strange that something so beautiful could be so deadly.

And then, I began to wonder. *After all this hardship, after killing so many people…could my heart still be pure?* Heart racing, I raised a hand.

August bolted up and gripped my wrist before I could touch the orb, his eyes narrowed. "Don't."

I studied his face, his pleading eyes. "I have to know," I whispered.

"Is the knowledge worth dying for?"

I didn't reply.

His gaze lingered on my face for a moment, and then he pried his fingers from my arm and stepped back.

I turned my attention onto the plant, and just before I touched it, I closed my eyes and said a prayer. *Lord...forgive me. For everything I've ever done wrong, forgive me.*

My fingertips brushed against the orb, surprising me with its coldness. What appeared to be glass was actually ice.

I waited...but nothing happened. I cracked open my eyes and dropped my hand.

August was visibly relieved. "Well...that was brave. Now you know."

And then the pain hit.

I doubled over, clutching my arm.

August crouched down beside me, voice frantic as he said, "Ivy? What's wrong?"

I wasn't able to answer, but I knew what was happening. I'd felt this pain before, like a knife carving slowly through my skin, going round and round my arm. Pain so piercingly unbearable that I teetered on the threshold of unconsciousness.

I lay there, writhing on the ground, until it finally stopped, leaving me panting and breathless on the icy floor, black dots spotting my vision.

I looked at August, who was now staring at my arm. I followed his gaze down to the scar that now creeped around my bicep, all the way to the elbow.

His eyes flicked back up to mine. "Are you okay?"

I nodded and rubbed my tingling arm. "I am now."

"Why did that happen?"

The answer was simple. The plant had given me too much power for a mortal body. But all I said was, "I-I think it was a warning."

August helped me up, his hand almost as ice-cold as the floor itself. "A warning?"

I traced the mutilated skin that had already healed into an ugly pink line. "It means I don't have long. To save my brother, to save the kingdoms...to live."

He grimaced. "Why? Why would it affect you that way and not me?"

I don't know. I shrugged. "Maybe because you have the orb. Or maybe you consumed enough to actually be immortal."

His face darkened and then he closed his eyes, his brow furrowed in concentration.

My power was sucked away from me, and the light around us turned to shadow as my body shifted into first form. I felt suddenly cold and weak. "Why did you do that?"

In the dim moonlight that filtered in through the gap, I could barely see him.

His eyes flickered back open, pale and ghostlike in the darkness. "If you don't have power, it can't hurt you."

For the first time ever, I was grateful for his strange ability to control who shifted around him. It would give me more time. *I just wished he'd asked first.*

Even so, it gave me an idea. I glanced at the plant. "I think I know how we can defeat King Ciaran."

"How is that?" he asked.

"When I went to rescue my brother, I couldn't. Your father has too many men, too many sorcerers." He nodded and crossed his arms. "But if we bring the orb, you can absorb their power."

"And then, we can rescue your brother and kill my father," he finished. "But...I don't know if it's possible. I've never tried to control that many people at once."

My heart sank, and I turned my head away.

He rested his hands on my shoulders, making me look back up into his eyes.

"I didn't say I wouldn't try it, though," he said, his mouth formed into a small smile. "It's the best plan we've come up with yet."

The corners of my mouth pulled up slightly in return. "So…what's the rest of the plan? When do we leave?"

His face darkened as he dropped his hands to his sides and led the way in the direction of the shelters. I followed closely, and soon, we were both looking out at the scorched ruins of the camp. Wails echoed through the gap as people discovered their loved ones. How many lives had been lost? How many people left grieving and wounded?

August's eyes shimmered with unshed tears. He grit his teeth with the effort to keep them from falling. When he spoke, his voice was grave and yet, at the same time, resounding with passion. "We'll recover. We'll move camp. And then, we'll kill King Ciaran."

THE END
OF BOOK TWO.

-ACKNOWLEDGMENTS-

I've been so blessed to have many, many people who have contributed in some way to my writing and my books.

I express my gratitude to:

Sierra Istre, Sarah Mitchell, David Mitchell, Thomas Gauthier, Mom, and Hannah for tireless hours of editing.

The Tung Family, for their support and encouragement at the local library's "write-ins". Can't wait for November!

My family, my friends, and my church family who have encouraged, uplifted, and inspired me.

Cassandra Boyson, fellow author, for our emailing friendship.

Widhi Saputro, for incredibly creative artwork for the covers of both Spark and Icebound.

My readers, who have supported me and encouraged me as I develop as a writer. You guys are awesome!

Lastly, but most importantly, to God. Without the beauty of the earth and the gift of music, I would lack the inspiration to write.

-ABOUT THE AUTHOR-

J.B. NORTH grew up in central Texas where she spent her time scouring the bookshelves in her aunt's school library. She published her first book, *Spark (Legends of the Shifters: Book One)*, when she was seventeen years old. She enjoys drawing badly, singing, and watching BBC television.

North now lives in southern Virginia, where she spends her days writing and caring for people's pups.

Find out more about J.B. North by visiting her website at AuthorJBNorth.com.

47484546R00199

Made in the USA
San Bernardino, CA
31 March 2017